U0754819

ZHONGGUO WENHUA MIANMIANGUAN

中国文化面面观

岁月痕迹　抚今追昔　地域风情

成　梅◎译

东北师范大学出版社
NORTHEAST NORMAL UNIVERSITY PRESS

长春

图书在版编目（CIP）数据

中国文化面面观：英文 / 鲁迅等著；成梅译 . —
长春：东北师范大学出版社，2017.1

ISBN 978 - 7 - 5681 - 1259 - 8

Ⅰ. ①中… Ⅱ. ①鲁…②成… Ⅲ. ①散文集—中国
—现代—英文②散文集—中国—当代—英文 Ⅳ. ①I266

中国版本图书馆 CIP 数据核字（2017）第 041238 号

□策划编辑：王春彦 　　　　　□封面设计：中联学林
□责任编辑：成　梅　王春彦 　□内文设计：中联学林
□责任校对：许寅逸 　　　　　□责任印制：张 允 豪

东北师范大学出版社出版发行

长春市净月开发区金宝街 118 号（邮政编码：130117）

销售热线：0431 - 84568122

传真：0431 - 84568122

网址：http：//www. nenup. com

电子函件：sdcbs@ mail. jl. cn

北京天正元印务有限公司印装

2017 年 5 月第 1 版　2017 年 5 月第 1 次印刷

幅面尺寸：170mm×240mm　印张：12.5　字数：225 千

定价：**38.00** 元

目 录
CONTENTS

Part III

2

Part I

Childhood Nurse and the Ancient Books
On Cultural Geography

Lu Xun

Mum Long[1] was a woman servant in my family who had taken care of me, or, in more ostentatious terms, my childhood nurse. My mother and many others called her Mum Long to show a sort of politeness. The only exception was my grandma who called her Ah Long. I normally called her Ah Mum. However, when I was angry at her, for example, when I knew she had murdered my pet mole, I would call her Ah Long.

Actually, there was nobody with the family name "Long" in our neighborhood; nor was "long" the adjective to describe her since she was short and stout. I remember once she told me her maiden name, which had nothing to do with "Long," though I cannot recall what it was. She also told me why she was called Ah Long: years before, there had been a very tall woman servant in my family, so the word "long" was just her nickname. When this tall servant quitted, my nurse, whatever she was called at that time, took her place. As everyone in my family was already accustomed to calling the woman doing this job "Long," she had ever since become Mum Long.

Although it is not good to make captious comments about others behind their backs, I cannot refrain from saying that I did not admire her at all, to tell the truth. The most loathsome thing about her was that she liked nothing more than whispering endlessly to others, with her forefinger waving up and down or pointing at the listener's nose or her own. Whenever disturbances arose in the household, I irresistibly suspected that these were somehow related to her whispering. I disliked her also because she forbade me to move about. If I pulled up a weed or turned over a small piece of stone, she would scold me for being naughty and tell my mother all about it. Summer nights, she had a habit of sprawling like a Chinese character "大" right in the middle of the matted bed. This left me only a narrow, sunned edge of the straw mat, so narrow that I found it difficult even to turn over in bed. Sometimes I tried to push her or wake her up, but all to no avail.

After hearing my complaints, my mother would say to her:

"Mum Long, you are a little too fat, and it must be difficult for you to resist the hot summer and sleep in a decent way? ..."

I knew this was a reminder that she should give me more room at night. Yet, silence was usually her only response. The following night when I woke from unbearable heat, I saw again that the whole bed was occupied by her sprawling heavy body, and one of her arms lay right on my neck! Hopelessly, I had to accept this kind of situation.

Moreover, she knew a lot of customs, with which I could not be patient enough. On New Year's Eve, the most happy time of the year, we children would get some money wrapped in red paper from the seniors after the ceremony of bidding farewell to the outgoing year. The money we got could be spent freely from the following day on. For the time being, we would lie on the bed, eyeing from time to time the money in the red paper beside the pillow and thinking of all the good things that could be bought the next day: the small drum, the toy knife and gun, the clay figure, and the sugar Bodhisattva... While I was still excitedly planning, Mum Long suddenly broke in and put a "lucky tangerine", actually the reddish orange produced in Fujian Province (In Chinese, "fu" in Fujian can mean "lucky"—the translator), beside my pillow.

"Brother," in great solemnity she said to me, "tomorrow is the first day of a new lunar year. Remember well when you open your eyes in the early morning, the first word to say to me should be: 'Mum, congratulations!' Don't forget. This concerns the whole year's luck. Don't say anything else. After you say what I tell you, eat the tangerine." With that, she took up the tangerine and waved it before my eyes. "In this way, everything will go smoothly during the whole year..."

That night, I even dreamed of the New Year's Day. The following morning I awoke very early. I was about to sit up, but Mum Long stretched out her hand and pressed me down. I looked at her in surprise, and she, in turn, looked at me with anxiety. Then she began to shake my shoulders, as if she wanted me to do something.

All of a sudden, I remembered—"Congratulations, Mum."

"Congratulations! Congratulations! You're a clever boy!" She looked very happy and inserted something cool into my mouth. I was taken aback for a moment and then realized it must be the "lucky tangerine." Till then, I was finally through with the procedure of beginning the new year and got the permission to get off the bed to play.

Besides these, she also taught me many life lessons. For instance, she told me if a person died, never say "He's dead," but say "He's going to his resting place." At another time she said it was not good to go to a room where a person had just died or a baby was just born. The third les-

son she gave me was that we should pick up and eat every grain of rice fall-
en on the ground at the meal time. Still another thing was that under no
circumstances should a child pass under a bamboo pole on which a pair of
trousers was hung drying in the sun. There were many other things which
have already escaped me, only the queer ceremony for the new year remains in my memory as clearly as ever. How ridiculous and tedious it was!
Just remembering it, I still find it troublesome.

But occasionally, my admiration even extended to her. She often told
me of "the long-haired men." What she called long-haired men not only
included Hong Xiuquan's insurrectionary peasant army which rose in the
middle of the 19th century, but also covered all the later bandits and rob-
bers. Only the revolutionary party was not counted, because there weren't
such men at her time. She described the long-haired men as terrible people
whose language was difficult to understand. According to her, my family
fled to the seaside, leaving only a doorkeeper and an old woman cook to
take care of the house upon hearing of the coming of the long-haired men.
When these men arrived at the town and entered our house, the old woman
called them "Your Majesty"—it was said one had to address the long-haired men in this way—and told them she was hungry. These men threw at
her a round thing with a pig tail—the head of the doorkeeper—and
laughed: "Go to cook and eat it!" The old woman was scared out of her
wits and whenever this was mentioned, she would look very ashen and keep
tapping her chest while crying: "Oh, how terribly dreadful, how terribly
dreadful it was…"

But I seemed not to have been infected by her fear, for I was not the
doorkeeper anyway, and the whole affair had nothing to do with me. Probably knowing what I was thinking, she added, "The long-haired men also

6

captured children like you to raise as little long-haired men. Good-looking girls were taken prisoners too. "

"Then, you'll be left undisturbed. " I thought she would be the safest since she was neither a doorkeeper nor a child. Besides, she had many scars on her neck, which made her plain face even less attractive.

"What nonsense!" she said gravely. "How can you think that we have no use. They caught us and let us stand in lines on the city wall with our pants down when the enemy attacked. It was said this would make the enemy cannon unable to fire. If they insisted on firing, the shell would explode inside the bore of the cannon!"

This was quite beyond my expectations, and I could not help but feel astonished. All along I thought she merely had some knowledge of some troublesome ceremonies and etiquettes without the least idea that she had such magic power. From then on, I began to have some respect for her, a really unfathomable woman. For this, her sprawling occupation of the whole bed at night seemed quite reasonable. It was I who should give in.

However, as the days passed by, my respect for her diminished little by little. The total oblivion of it came with the revelation that she was the murderer of my pet mole. I questioned her gravely on this and called her Ah Long face to face. Since I was not caught to be a little long-haired man and I would not be attacking the city or firing a gun, hence not in danger of experiencing the shell exploding inside the bore of the cannon, why should I fear her?

While I was grieving over my pet's death and thinking of taking my revenge for it, my attention was somehow drawn to *Shan Hai Jing*, a set of ancient classic books on cultural geography. My longing for these books was actually incited by my distant grand-uncle. He was a fat, kindly old man, whose hobby was horticulture and he cultivated a variety of flowers, such as zhulan tree, jasmine and the rare lantana, which was said to have been brought from the north. His wife was just the opposite of him, unable to make heads or tails of anything. She once put the bamboo pole for sunning clothes on the branch of the zhulan tree. The branch broke, and she cursed angrily: "Damn it!" My grand-uncle was hence very lonely. Having nobody to talk with, he made friends with us children. In the residence where all the members of our clan lived, he was the one who possessed the biggest collection of books, including some rather unique copies. Books on eight-part essays and poems for imperial examination were certainly among his collection, but I saw in his study Lu Ji's *Notes on All the Living Things in the Book of Songs* and other unfamiliar books. My favorite book was *Hua Jing*, a set of books with illustrations on gardening written in the Qing Dynasty. The old man told me there had been a set of books called *Shan Hai Jing*, which had many peculiar pictures in it, such as the beast with the human face, the snake with nine heads, the bird with three legs, the man with wings, the headless monster which used his breasts as eyes, etc. The problem was that he could not remember where he had put it.

My curiosity was greatly aroused by his description of the books, but I simply could not urge him to look for them for me, since he was a little careless and lazy by nature. I tried to consult others, but none could give me satisfactory answers. I then thought of buying the books with what was left of the money I had got from the seniors as a lunar New Year's gift, which still amounted to a few hundred *wen*. Yet, the street in which one could find bookstores was so far from where I lived that we could only go there during the traditional holidays of the first lunar month, which was unfortunately the time when the bookstores were all closed.

Apart from the time I concentrated on playing, I was haunted endlessly by the longing for such a set of books.

In due course, my constant hankering for the books became known to Ah Long, who came to ask questions about it, though I myself never informed her of this, thinking it was useless to tell this kind of thing to a woman who was no scholar at all. Now since she showed some concern for this, I told her all about my trouble.

Nearly a month later, that was about four or five days after she went home on leave as I can remember, she came back in a new blue cloth upper garment. Upon seeing me, she handed me a parcel of books and smiled brightly.

"Brother, here is the set of "San Heng Jing" with pictures. I bought it for you!"

This hit me like a thunderbolt. While stupefied by what she had done for me, I hurried to take hold of the parcel and unfolded the wrapping paper. It turned out to be a set of four small books. With a rough scan, I found it really contained the beast with a human face, the snake with nine heads...

A new admiration for her welled up in my heart. She had done what the others would not or could not do. She really had some magic power. By this time, my resentment against her for murdering the little mole had entirely passed into oblivion.

These four books were my earliest treasured possession. My memory of the appearance of the books is still as fresh as before. The books gave me an impression of something made with very rough and crude block printing. The paper was very yellow and the pictures were disfigured. Many of them were drawn with straight lines so that the eyes of the animals looked like rectangles. Anyhow, my appreciation of the set was not in the least affected by its poor workmanship, for it really had the beast with a human face, the snake with nine heads, the cow with only one leg, the bag-like bird, and the mythological figure—the headless giant Xing Tian, who, using his breasts as eyes and his navel as his mouth, and holding a shield in one hand and an ax in the other, danced wildly.

Ever since then, I had collected more books with illustrations. I had the lithographic sets of books, such as the three-copy set *The New Er Ya Dictionary with Phonetic Notes*, the seven-copy set *Illustrations and Explanations of the Living Things in the Books of Songs*, I also had the ten-copy set *Dian Shi Zhai Cong Hua—A Collection of Chinese Paintings*, and *Shi Hua Fang*, a collection of paintings of the Ming Dynasty in China. Moreover, I bought a new set of *Shan Hai Jing* in lithographic printing. They were books in reduced format with notes provided by Hao Yixing, a much more exquisite set than the block-printed edition. Poems accompanying illustrations were found in every volume, the pictures being printed in green and the characters in red. I had kept the lithographic set until very recently, whereas the block-printed set has long since been lost.

My nurse, Mum Long (or Ah Long) passed away about thirty years ago. I never got to know her name or her experiences. All I know about her life is that she had an adopted son. From this I guess she might be a widow who lost her husband early in her youth.

May her soul rest forever in the dark bosom of the benevolent mother earth!

The translator's notes:

1. "Long" here means "tall" in some dialect of southern China.

About the author: Lu Xun (1881 – 1936) was the most prominent modern writer and thinker in China.

About the essay: Through this recollection devoted to his childhood nurse, Lu Xun gives vivid descriptions of a typically uneducated working woman in China at the end of the nineteenth century, who somehow was a carrier of the traditional Chinese folk culture.

From the Grass Garden to the Three-flavor Study

Lu Xun

Behind my parents' former house there was a large garden plot which used to be called the Grass Garden. Now the garden, together with the house, has been sold to the Zhu family, probably the descendants of Zhu Xi, the famous philosopher and educator in the Southern Song Dynasty. It has been seven or eight years since I saw the garden for the last time. It consisted of only several kinds of grasses, but it was once as good as a paradise to me.

Apart from the dark green vegetable beds, the well surrounded by a glossy stone railing, the tall Chinese honey locust tree, the purplish red mulberry, the long chirps of cicadas in the tree leaves, the fleshy wasps on the cauliflowers, and the spry and light skylark suddenly flying up like an arrow from the grass into the cloud, the place around the foot of the mud wall alone was already infinitely interesting to me—the small black beetles were singing and the crickets seemed to be accompanying on the piano. Turning a broken brick over, you sometimes found a centipede or a cantharis, which would give out a whiff of smoke from its rear end upon being pressed. The vine of multiflower knotweed was intertwined with that of magnolia, which bore fruit much like a shower nozzle. It was said that the tuber of multiflower knotweed resembled a human figure, and if a human being ate it regularly, he would become immortal. I used to pull out the multiflower knotweed together with the root; even if the pulling might do harm to the mud wall, yet I never found a root that really looked like the human figure. And, if one was not afraid of the thorns, he could pick the fruit of the Korean raspberry, which was a cluster of tart and sweet beads, much better than the mulberry both in color and in taste.

However, we never dared to go into the tall grass in the garden, for according to the legend there was a large red-striped snake hidden in it.

Mum Long once told me a story: long, long ago, there was a scholar who lodged in an ancient temple and studied diligently. One summer evening, when he was enjoying the coolness in the courtyard, he suddenly heard someone call him. He answered and looked around, and caught sight of the smiling face of a beauty hidden behind the wall, but it soon disappeared. He felt very pleased until he met the old monk later. The monk said he looked as if being enchanted by some evil spirit; he must have met the "snake beauty," a monster that had a human head but the body of a snake. It could call a man's name, and if he answered, it would return at night and eat him. The scholar was then very scared, but the monk told him not to be worried, and gave him a small box to put beside his pillow. In this way, as the monk added, everything would be all right. The scholar did what he was told, but still could not fall asleep. This was natural for a man in such a situation. Sure enough, at midnight the monster arrived and there was much swishing and rustling outside the door, like the sound of wind and rain. While the scholar was trembling with fear, a beam of golden light jetted from beside the pillow. Immediately nothing could be heard outside. Then the light flew back into the box. The monk explained later that the thing in the box was called a flying centipede, which could suck the brains of the monster, thus killing it.

The lesson that could be drawn from this story was that one should never answer if his name was being called by a stranger.

The story also gave me a sense of danger in life. From then on, when I cooled myself outside in summer evenings, I was always worried, and dared not look at the top of the wall. I wished that I had a box of flying centipedes as the old monk had. When I passed the thick growth of grass in the garden, similar feelings occurred. Yet to this day, I have never obtained a box of flying centipedes, nor have I seen a red-striped snake or a snake-beauty. I often heard strange voices calling my name, but none of them came from a snake beauty.

The grass garden in winter was relatively dull, except when it snowed. Yet, the game played on snow days was not that of imprinting one's figure in the snow or of making an *arhat*[1] with snow. Since it was a deserted garden, few would come to appreciate this kind of thing. Hence, catching birds was what we often indulged in there. To do this, we had to wait until a fairly heavy snow covered the ground for one or two days, so that there was nowhere for birds to look for food for some time. At this time one would choose a spot and sweep the snow away, and fix a big bamboo sieve supported by a short rod on the cleared ground. Then blighted grains of rice were scattered under the sieve and a long rope was fastened to the rod. People watched at a distance with the other end of rope in hand. Upon seeing some birds walk under the sieve and peck at the grains, one would draw the rope, so that the sieve collapsed with the birds enclosed beneath it. The captured birds were mostly sparrows. Sometimes, white-faced wagtails were found to have been caught, too, but they were restless birds,

14

which could hardly be kept alive overnight.

This method of catching birds as taught to me by Run Tu's father proved unsuccessful. Even if I saw for sure that many birds had entered the area under the sieve, there were rarely any caught beneath it after I yanked the rope and ran to the sieve to see what I had. It usually would take me an entire half a day to catch three or four birds; whereas, with less time, Run Tu's father could have several dozen birds cheeping and fluttering around in his bag. I once asked him the reason for his success and my failure. He smiled quietly and said: "You should have waited until the birds got further under the sieve. "

My family would soon send me off to a private school, the strictest in town. I could not understand why they had arrived at such a decision. Maybe it was because I had ruined the mud wall when pulling out the multiflower knotweed, or because I had once thrown a broken brick into the neighboring house of the Liang family, or because I had stood on the stone railing of the well and jumped down... In any case, I would not be able to come to the grass garden often. Goodbye, my crickets! Goodbye, my Korean raspberries and magnolias!

Stepping out of my parents' house, I would walk about half a Chinese *li* (one Chinese *li* equals to 500 meters—the translator) and cross a stone bridge to get to my teacher's house whose entrance was a bamboo gate painted black. Passing through it, one would soon reach the third room, which served as the study. In the middle of the study was hung a horizontal board with the following words inscribed on it: Three-flavor Study. Below the board was a picture of a large sika deer lying prostrate under an ancient tree. Since there was no memorial tablet of Confucius, we new pupils just saluted the board and the deer. The first salute was meant for Confucius, the second for the teacher.

The teacher answered our second salute amiably. He was a tall and thin old man with white hair, a white beard, and a pair of big glasses. I was very respectful of him, for I had long heard that he was very upright, simple, honest and learned.

I had also heard somewhere that Dongfang Shuo, a well-known writer in the Western Han Dynasty, had been very learned, too. He knew of a kind of insect called "Strange," which was the incarnation of un-redressed injustice and could be dissolved if one poured alcohol on it. I had wanted very much to know the details of the story. But Ah Long, my childhood nurse knew nothing about it, for, after all, she was not educated. Now I had the chance—I could ask the teacher about it.

"Sir, what kind of insect is 'Strange'?" I asked when the class for new lessons was coming to the end.

"I don't know!" He appeared very displeased, almost on the verge of anger.

Only at this time did I come to know that a pupil should not ask such questions, but instead work on his lessons. My teacher was a very learned intellectual, and it could not be possible that he didn't know this. The truth was that he did not want to tell me about it. Some of my seniors behaved in this way, and I had experienced this behavior several times before.

So I read all day long, took some handwriting exercises at noon, and practiced antithesis-making drills in the evening. For the first several days, the teacher was very strict with me. Later he softened, but assigned greater numbers of books to me. And the poems we read had more and more Chinese characters in each line: from three to five and from five to seven.

There was also a garden behind the Three-flavor Study. Small as it was, we could at least climb on the flower terrace and snap some branches with wintersweets on them, or look on the ground and on the osmanthus tree for cicada slough. Our best work in the garden, however, was feeding ants with captured flies. It was a soundless game. However, if too many pupils came to the garden to linger for too long, the teacher would shout in the study:

"Where is everybody?"

On hearing this, we had to return to the study one by one—it was no good for us to come back together. He kept a ruler for beating pupils, though seldom used it. He had a rule of penalty kneeling, which was also rarely observed. Usually he gazed at us and called out loudly:

"Read!"

This set everyone into a roar of reading aloud and the study was filled with a hubbub of voices. We read aloud various extracts from the ancient classics. But some read aloud without punctuating the sentences, thus making them indiscernible; some just meddled with the word order of the sentences and reduced the reading to totally meaningless noises. The teacher himself would read aloud, too. Later, our voices became lower and weaker until, coming to a stand still, only his voice was heard as loud as ever:

With the iron ruyi, he surprised all present with his elegant dictation;

*With the gold cup, he drank to his heart's content without getting intox-*icated.

I guess these sentences must be very well written, for whenever he read them, he would smile brightly and raise his head, nodding slightly.

When the teacher was engrossed in his reading, we would have a good time. Some pupils made miniature helmets out of paper and placed them on their fingers and let them represent the army men fighting each other. I usually took advantage of the time by drawing pictures. I put the translucent Jingchuan paper on the exquisitely drawn portraits in the classic novels and traced them one by one, just as we often did in the writing class—laying a printed model copy beneath a piece of similarly translucent paper and tracing each character with a writing brush on the paper. The more I read, the more pictures I drew. It seemed that I had made much more progress in picture-drawing than in reading. The bulk of my pictures was made from the two popular classic novels *Will to Wipe Out the Bandits* and *The Pilgrimage to the West*. Each novel was heavily illustrated with pictures of the story's characters. Later, when I was in need of money, I sold my tracings to a classmate whose rich father kept a tinfoil paper shop. It is said now that he has taken over the shop and will soon become a gentleman. The collections of tracings I sold to him may have long been lost.

The translator's notes:

1. *Arhat* is a word in Sanskrit, referring to the monk who has freed himself from all desires, cares and worries.

About the author: Lu Xun (1881 – 1936) was the most prominent modern writer and thinker in China.

About the essay: It was first published in 1926 in Issue 19 of *Mang Yuan* (*Steppe*). It is more a revelation of China's traditional way of elementary education than the childhood recollection.

The Spring Festival of Beijing

Lao She

It was the traditional custom of Beijing that the Lunar New Year—The Spring Festival—began from the first ten days of the twelfth month of the lunar year. As the old saying goes: "Even the jackdaw is frozen to death on the seventh or eighth day of the last lunar month," the twelfth month is the coldest time of the year. Knowing that spring follows closely the severe winter, people have never lost enthusiasm for celebrating the festival to welcome the new spring no matter how cold the weather is. On the eighth day of the last lunar month of each year, every family, temple or monastery would cook a special kind of porridge as an offering to gods or ancestors. The offering was a proud manifestation of the agricultural society, as the porridge was made of various kinds of rice, beans, peas, nuts and dried fruit, say, apricot kernels, walnut meat, shelled peanuts, water chestnuts and water melon seeds, dried litchi, lotus seeds, raisin, etc. The porridge was truly a miniature agricultural exhibit!

Also on the eighth day of the last lunar month, people would soak garlic cloves in vinegar and then seal the container. At the end of the year, every garlic clove would look as transparent as jadeite while the vinegar smelled of the pungent garlic. This was made to be the sauce for meat and vegetable dumplings on New Year's Eve, and would whet people's appetite greatly. In Beijing every family ate dumplings on New Year's Eve.

From the eighth day of the last lunar month, every store would try to replenish more and sell more. Stalls would appear on the street selling Spring Festival couplets, pictures, candied fruit and narcissus. Especially meant for the festival, the stalls would always quicken the heart beats of the children. Inside the alleys, the shouts of the vendors would seem to be more diverse than usual, including shouts selling the constitution book, the pine branch, the seeds of Job's tears, and the New Year cake. These shouts can only be heard during the twelfth lunar month.

At the time when the country was under the regime of the emperors, school began vacation on the 19th of the twelfth lunar month and lasted a month for the festival. The first thing the children did to prepare for the New Year's Day was to buy the assorted preserved fruit, which included shelled peanuts, dates saturated with sugar, hazelnuts, chestnuts, etc. and various candied fruit. The low-price mixes were made of unshelled nuts and the high-price, only the meats of the nuts. Children were so fond of the assorted preserved fruit that they placed buying this kind of food before anything else, even before eating dumplings. The second important thing for the children, especially for the boys, was buying firecrackers; and the third, buying playthings—kites, diabolos, mouth organs, etc. and the New Year's pictures.

Not only did children bustle about, but adults also were busy preparing everything needed during the festival. They hurried to finish the new clothes and new shoes for the children so they could look smart and fashionable on New Year's Day.

The twenty-third of the twelfth lunar month was called the Preliminary

New Year, and was a "dress rehearsal" of the formal New Year's Day. In the old society, every family made sacrifices to the Kitchen God on this evening. As soon as it was getting dark, while the sound of firecrackers rang through the city, people would burn the picture of the Kitchen God "to send him up into Heaven". Several days before that, vendors in the streets would sell malt sugar and sweets made of glutinous rice in the shape of cuboids or gourds, big or small. Tradition told that if the mouth of the Kitchen God was glued together by such sticky sugar, he would not be able to speak ill of the family before the Jade Emperor when he reached Heaven. Today, the sugar seller can still be found, only the sugar and sweets are no longer used to stick the mouth of the Kitchen God, but rather for everyone's enjoyment.

When the twenty-third was over, everyone was even busier, for the New Year's Day was quickly arriving. One must clean thoroughly and paste the Spring Festival couplets on the gateposts or door panels. Moreover, they must shop for and prepare meat, chicken, fish, vegetables, and cakes for family feasts during the one week holidays. All the stores and shops would close for at least five days till the sixth of the first lunar month, and if one did not have enough food to last all these days, people could find nowhere to buy more in time of need. Furthermore, according to the old women in the old society, everything that needed to be chopped in a few days to come should be chopped on the New Year's Eve so as to avoid taking up a chopping knife from the first day to the fifth day of the first lunar month, for during that time, it was not auspicious to touch a knife or a pair of scissors. Superstitious as it was, this notion at least shows that the Chinese people are peace-loving people, who tried to avoid touching even the kitchen knife at the beginning of every year.

21

New Year's Eve was full of excitement, bustle and activities. Every family was busy with the food and dishes for the festival and every place smelled of delicious meat and wine. All people, old and young, men and women, were dressed in new clothes. Red couplets were pasted on the front doors of the houses and various New Year's pictures were affixed on the walls inside the rooms. Every family kept their lights ablaze all through the night and firecrackers could be heard day and night. The family members who worked away from home were sure to come back to have the family reunion dinner and offer sacrifices to the ancestors unless it was absolutely necessary for them to remain where they were. During the whole night, everyone except little babies stayed up all night for the New Year's Eve.

New Year's Day was completely different from New Year's Eve: on the eve, the streets were full of people, whereas on New Year's Day, every shop or store was shut, with paper pieces from the firecrackers used last night piling here and there before the closed doors. The whole city was taking a rest.

Men usually set off on trips to the homes of their relatives or friends to pay a New Year call while women stayed at home to receive guests. The temples and monasteries inside and outside of the city were all open and could be freely visited and toured. Vendors set their stalls outside these places selling tea, food and all kinds of toys. The Big Bell Temple to the north of the city, the White Cloud Temple to the west of the city and the Temple for the Fire God in the south of the city were among the most famous resorts. On the very first two or three days when the temples were open to the public, the spots were not as lively as in later days, for people were still busy paying New Year's calls to each other and could spare no time for sightseeing. It was not until the fifth or sixth day of the new year that the temple fairs became real attractions. Children were especially eager to go to the fairs, both for sightseeing on donkey back out of the city and for the toys that could only be found during the festival. On the square before the White Cloud Temple, there were horse races and carriage races. It was said that years earlier, there had even been camel races. In these races, the results or places were not taken into any account, but rather, it was the graceful posture and feats of the performing men and horses that really mattered to the onlookers.

Most of the shops and stores reopened on the sixth day of the first lunar month. Strings of small firecrackers were again lighted, and the crackling and spluttering sound rang in the city from daybreak to the early morning. Still, except those that sold food and other necessities, the shops and stores had few customers. Consequently, the assistants could take turns to visit the temple fairs or the overpass, another festive resort where people show all kinds of skills, or go to the opera.

With the appearance of the round sweet dumplings on the market, arrived the climax of the New Year's celebration, and that was the Lantern Festival (from the thirteenth to the seventeenth of the first lunar month). New Year's Eve was exciting but moonless; whereas during the Lantern Festival, the bright full moon was right in the sky. New Year's Day was made festive by the red couplets pasted on the two sides of every door and the new clothes everyone wore, but it was not as beautiful as the Lantern Festival, during which every place was decorated with lanterns and colored streamers and there was a blaze of light and color in the streets. Some well-known stores with a long history would hang out hundreds of lanterns each. Lanterns hung by one store might all be made of glass, by another all made of ox horn, still another all made of gauze, while some stores preferred lanterns of all kinds or had the stories of *A Dream of Red Mansions* or *The Waterside* painted on the lanterns. All this, during old times, was a kind of advertisement: the hanging lanterns would draw crowds of visitors, especially at night when all the lanterns were lighted. This was a really effective kind of advertisement. The store selling dried fruit always adopted some original designs and made various ice lanterns or used the wheat seedling to build one or two green dragons to attract customers in order that great quantities of the assorted preserved fruit could be sold during the Lantern Festival.

Flowerpots were also displayed on the square during the Lantern Festival. In the Town God's Temple the mud statue of a fire judge was enkindled and raging flames stretched out of its mouth, nose, ears and eyes. And in the parks, fireworks like huge stars were shot one by one into the sky.

Men and women all went out to enjoy the lanterns, the fireworks and the first full moon of the year. The streets were so crowded that people could hardly move. In the old society, women were seldom allowed to go out of their houses, but they had more freedom during the Lantern Festival.

Children usually bought a great variety of fireworks and firecrackers. Even if they didn't go out to play mischievously in the street, they could well occupy themselves with the special toys of sound and light. There were also lanterns at home: the lanterns with paper-cut figures of men, animals, etc. which could revolve when the lanterns were lit—a rather primitive film, as well as the palace lanterns, paper lanterns of all kinds, and gauze lanterns with small bells in them, ringing regularly. And every family made and ate the round sweet dumplings on this day. This was really the day full of pleasure and delight.

In the twinkling of the eye, the time came when the temple fairs and lantern displays drew to their ends and children had to go to school and adults attend to their work and business. The New Year's celebration at last ended on the 19th of the first lunar month. The twelfth month and the beginning month of another lunar year were the idlest months for everyone in the agricultural society, and also the months in which pigs, cows and sheep were fattened up for the butcher. People were thus rewarded for their year's hard work. When the Lantern Festival was over, the weather began to get warmer and warmer, and people began to return to their work. Although Beijing was a city, it celebrated the New Year's Day together with the agricultural society and observed the customs in a lively way.

Of course, superstition was involved in the celebration of New Year's Day in the old society. When the porridge of the eighth day of the twelfth month, the malt candy and dumplings for the New Year's Eve were made, they were first offered to the Buddha and were then enjoyed by the people. Ceremonies were held to welcome and receive gods on New Year's Eve and sacrifices offered to the God of Wealth on the second day of the new year. This day was also the time to make *won ton*, the dumpling soup to symbolize the gold and silver ingots—the money used in ancient China. Meanwhile, some people would go to the Temple of the God of Wealth to borrow ingots made of paper and compete to burn the first joss sticks. On the eighth day of the new year, people would pray for felicity and longevity. For all the events, a great deal of money was wasted on the joss sticks, candles, and all kinds of paper things needed for the offerings. Nowadays, as people are no longer superstitious, these expenses are saved for more useful things. It is worth mentioning that the children today, without being influenced by the superstitious ceremonies, can celebrate the New Year more happily. They need no longer to worry about the gods and ghosts, but enjoy the gaiety fully. Maybe today's New Year celebrations are not as exciting as before, yet they are more healthy and rational. In the old days, people depended on the protection of gods and ghosts to celebrate the New Year; today people can enjoy the merry New Year's festivities that they deserve as a reward for their whole year's labor.

The translator's notes:

About the author: Lao She (1899 – 1966) was one the five most prominent modern novelist and playwright in China. He was once the vice-chair of the Chinese Writers Association.

About the essay: It was first published in 1951 in *New Observers* (Issue 2) in Beijing. This is a detailed account of the traditional Spring Festival celebration in Beijing, which is typical of northern China. Nowadays, some customs (say, avoiding using Kitchen knife in the first five days of the lunar year) are seldom observed.

Spring Festival Couplets

Lao She

To celebrate the Spring Festival, one should paste couplets. The couplets, written in shining black ink on bright red paper, to be pasted on gate posts or door panels, each on one side, would indeed enhance the jubilation. The content of the couplets used to be meaningful, ranging from spring praising to morale boosting. However, the form is quite unique, and it can only be created by the Chinese language. Every word in the first line must be antithetical to another word in the same position in the second one, the number of the characters (words) must be identical just like the length of one's legs should be the same in order to stand steadily. Couplets formed in this way really make people feel comfortable. Therefore, to create Spring Festival couplets is to exercise one's use of words since the two lines in the couplets should at least be antithetical, any ill match, say, one "boot" and one "shoe", will never be allowed in such a case.

Let me do the exercise according to this basic rule.

My first couplet concerns with the striking calendar feature of this Spring Festival: the New Year's Eve happens to be the day of the Beginning of Spring. This can be said to be dual jubilation, which is worth of special celebration. Hence the couplet can be made as follows:

The same day for both the Spring Festival and the Beginning of Spring

Every minute is precious for making progress as the occasion demands

Although this couplet is not good enough in antithesis, I believe it expresses well my mood of welcoming the spring. With the coming spring, every one should summon up all one's courage and energy and vie with each other in order to achieve more than last year.

My second couplet is for my son and my daughters:

Arrange work and rest properly to keep healthy and happy

Be industrious and thrifty in managing your own household

I want to see each of them full of vigor when working, while hoping that they all know how to strike a proper balance between work and rest and pay attention to their health so that they can prevent fatigue caused by overwork and are able to continue to work hard. I know they are all thrifty, so my second line just means to tell them to consolidate that good habit and make it a family tradition.

I want to give one couplet to Beijing People's Art Theatre:

All the people demand good plays

Higher level in Art is to be attained

I should give a couplet to The Chinese Youth's Art Theatre as well since both theatrical companies are my good friends:

Ride the wind and cleave the waves to have boundless prospects

Subdue the dragon and tame the tiger with soaring enthusiasm

This couplet may somehow sound too violent. As a couplet does not allow any note, I think it better to make the horizontal hanging scroll to match the couplet as "happy and relaxed". Is it a good solution?

I have already written a couplet for the poet Zang Kejia and sent it to him. However, as I cannot find the time to rub the ink stick on the ink slab to prepare ink for the brush writing, I have not actually written all the other couplets I mentioned here on red paper. As Kejia is always eager to learn and straightforward, my couplet for him is as follows:

Learning makes one modest

The writing mirrors the writer.

Finally, I will write a couplet for myself:

Writing requires tremendous effort

Guarding against piecing together

When writing, the worst thing is to piece together parts of the previously existing writings. To guard against this kind of practice, one must try one's best to revise a piece of writing again and again. When revision is not possible, then one has to rewrite the whole piece. Sometimes one even has to rewrite several times, which I cannot often do. When I am busy, I will have to hand in the imperfect piece of writing. Obviously, I should amend this tendency.

When I was in my teenage, I often went to help the old-style school teacher and the senior fellow students who used to set up a stall in the market selling couplets before the Spring Festival. My task was to rub the ink stick on the ink slab to prepare ink for the brush writing and to stretch the paper in order that they can write smoothly. They all have a couplet book that contains couplets of different categories. They would write them down on the red paper and put in place by categories. When buyers came and asked for a couplet for the Kitchen God or for the Door God, etc. , they would present the previously written ones accordingly, bargain for a good price and then sell them. Therefore, at that time it was a common scene that quite a number of families in the neighborhood got the same couplet "Heaven and man both grow older/Spring and happiness befall everywhere" on their door panels. Almost all families would have the couplet "Go to Heaven to tell the good news/Ensure people's safety when staying on earth" for the niches for the Kitchen God. Ever since 1949, people in Beijing have begun to create new Spring Festival couplets and reject clichés. This can certainly be regarded as a progress. To mention this in passing is to show that we don't need to stress the past. The present may be better.

The translator's notes:

About the author: Lao She (1899 – 1966) was one the five most prominent modern novelist and playwright in China. He was once the vice-chair of the Chinese Writers Association.

About the essay: This essay was published in *Beijing Daily*, February 3, 1962. Obviously, the new couplets he wrote reflected the spirit and the fad of the age in China in 1960s. They are quite different from China's traditional couplets for Spring Festival.

On Eating

Xia Mianzun

For me, the very first thing the Spring Festival stands for is food. When I was a child, I would eagerly look forward to the festival as soon as winter arrived. The closer the dates, the more I was overwhelmed with joy, for the festival always gave us much pleasure. Above all, there was always plenty to eat on this occasion.

The Chinese must be one of the peoples who are very good at eating in the world. In an ordinary family, when unexpected guests arrived, the host would immediately set out to get the necessary provisions while the hostess went to the kitchen to start the preparation of a family feast. The guests would just sit in the parlor, waiting for the dinner by cracking water melon seeds and listening to all the sounds of the busy cooking from the kitchen: the chopping, the clinking of bowls and dishes and so on. After the dinner had been served and finished, the guests would take their leave by saying, "Sorry to trouble you," and the host usually responded politely: "Sorry to have given you such a poor dinner." Some hosts would invite the guests to stay longer by giving suggestions: "Have some sweets and pastry", or "Please wait for the night refreshments."

Wedding or funeral ceremonies usually provide good pretexts for feasts, which can last from seven or five days down to three days or one day. Such a feast generally contains breakfast, lunch, afternoon refreshments, dinner, and night refreshments. Those who are present find great pleasure in having one meal after another and in seeing ponds of wine and forests of meat dishes.

On New Year's Eve, people take turns to have dinner with relatives or friends or send their home-made food to them. During the Spring Festival holidays, people pay the New Year call to each other and then sit at each other's feast tables. All through the year, people have sumptuous dinners on the 5th day of the 5th lunar month for the Dragon Boat Festival, on the 15th day of the 8th lunar month for the Mid-autumn Festival, on themselves' or others' birthdays and on the occasions of meeting or bidding farewell to their friends. In short, people find every possible excuse for a good dinner, which seems to be the ultimate end of whatever occasion.

A child may ask his or her mother for money several times a day just to eat between meals. For an ordinary pupil, the bulk of his expenses goes to various delicious snacks instead of tuition or book fees. In most cases, the presents that adults give their parents are composed of delicious foods. Ever since the ancient times, cuisine has been the essential lesson in the education of women. According to the traditional creeds on food, the meal cannot be too refined and the meat cannot be too minutely chopped; and wine cannot be drunk unless dried meat is bought. It is well known that the sage would not eat any meat "not rightly cut"; and the worthy man could renounce his wife if she was not able to steam pears to his taste. Until now, the proudest thing a man claims to have can be his wife's good recipes for food. All through history, many celebrated famous persons (not necessarily chefs—the translator) have racked their brains in creating or collecting original methods of cooking, which now consist of several sets of volumes.

Good food is not only meant for the living people, but for the dead in China. For other nations, the dead may be quite contented with the flowers sent to them; but for the Chinese, the dead must eat what the alive eat. Food is as important to the dead as when they were still alive, if not more important. Therefore, in old China, people spared neither labor nor money to obtain more good land and concubines in order to have good dishes sent to them when they were dead. For the cold pork to be sent to them before their graves, the Confucian moralists did their best to pretend to be benevolent and righteous all through their lives. Zhu Zhucha once relinquished his right to have the cold-dressing pork in order not to cut a love poem from his poetry anthology. The fact that this story has been passed from mouth to mouth with general approval as a rare example just shows that few people could make such a sacrifice.

In China, food should not only be given to the alive, to the dead, but also to the gods, even to the mountains and valleys without any mouth. Some of them are given the head of a pig, some a whole pig; some are offered sheep and some, cows—all their likings and preferences can be found in the ancient books on rites and etiquette. Compared with the foreign religious service meant for God, it seems that the foreign gods are rather idealistic, whereas the Chinese ones are really materialistic.

As said in Meicun's poem, "Three out of ten stores in the street are restaurants", food shops are found to be dominant in China's streets and markets. At home, the most troublesome thing is not education nor whatever else, but the preparation of food. At universities or colleges, people are not concerned with progress in studies or the improvement of teaching methods, but with unrest in the dining hall.

According to the common Chinese saying, only the two-legged ancestor and the four-legged bed cannot be eaten. The wide range of Chinese food can be really surprising to foreigners. Apart from what is common for people all over the world, the Chinese people regard as delicious the seeds of watermelon, the fins of sharks, and the nests of some kind of birds. They also eat dogs, tortoises, leopard cats, toads, soft-shelled turtles, small mice, and even the afterbirth of a baby or other things from the human body. If they could, they might have the moon cooked!

The ways of food preparation are of a wider variety: roasting, boiling, steaming, stewing, frying, braising, liquor-saturating, broiling, stir-frying, cold-dressing and so on. From the ancient times, many famous chefs have been crowned with eternal glory like important ministers and officials. Some of them really were given high positions and promoted to ministers or officials. If China has one thing to boast about to the world, it shouldn't be its long history, vast land, the biggest population or the multitudinous army, and the frequent wars, but its expertise in food preparation. The whole world has in fact been conquered by the Chinese food. It is said that the Chinese have "three knives" superior to those of other countries; the first one is the kitchen knife.

Have you ever seen the three-men picture representing happiness, emolument and longevity? These three things are actually the highest ideals of the Chinese nation. In the picture, the symbolization of emolument is in the middle, flanked by that of happiness on the right and that of longevity on the left. As a matter of fact, emolument has always been embodied by food. Laozi once said: "Man needs to have his stomach filled as well as remain modest", "The sage knows it is more important to feast one's stomach than to feast one's eyes. " Clearly the only thing that matters in the world for the Chinese is food. Among the old four enjoyments—going whoring, gambling, eating and dressing, eating is commonly regarded as the most materially beneficial. All could come to nothing except eating.

The Chinese language bears some evidences of the importance of eating. The word "eat" has such a wide and complicated range of meaning that it can be used to describe almost everything. Being bullied is "eating the wrongs", being boxed on the face is "eating a slap" and being hit by a shot "eating a pill. " To have a desire for something impossible is "to eat the swan's meat", and to be involved in a lawsuit is "to eat a lawsuit". There are also other expressions like "eating the life" (meaning that someone deserves to be beaten—the translator), "eating the file leader" (meaning that someone should be scolded—the translator) and so on. And instead of greeting others with "good morning", "good afternoon" and "good evening" like many foreign nations, the Chinese people use "have you eaten your breakfast", "have you eaten your lunch", and "have you eaten your supper" on the same occasions. What is more, a person's occupation is commonly told through the expression "eat a certain meal", such as "eat a gambler's meal", "eat a waiter's meal", "eat a foreign bank's meal", "eat a teacher's meal", etc. Even the follower of a religion and the defender of the country are described with the word "eat". For example, the Christian and Catholic are said to be persons eating Christian's meal and Catholic's meal respectively; and the army men are called "persons eating the grain. " Recently, some new expressions have been added to this list, among which are "eating the party's meal" and "eating the meal of the Three People's Principles[1]"

Food, clothing, shelter and transportation are basic necessities of life. Human beings simply cannot live without eating. Yet it is hard to find in the world a counterpart of the Chinese that have such complicated meanings attached to the word "eat," and make such an open demand for food and possess such wide scope and troublesome ways of eating. It seems that the only thing the Chinese care for is food.

People in China pay little attention to their dirty clothes, crude shelters, and muddy roads but never allow the food to be carelessly prepared. Among the four basic necessities of life, the refinement of food is much ahead of the other three in development and appears very incompatible. Consequently, the culture of the Chinese nation can be summed up as the culture of the mouth.

Buddhism divides the world into different sections of Heaven, man, Asura[2], animal, hell and hungry ghost. All the six make a whole cycle. If we believe in this, we may constantly have in mind the question as to whether or not the Chinese people are all the reincarnation of the hungry ghost.

The translator's notes:

1. The Three People's Principles refer to Nationalism, Democracy, and the People's Livelihood put forward by Dr. Sun Yetsen.

2. Asura is a Sanskrit word, referring to a kind of supernatural beings in ancient Indian myth.

About the author: Xia Mianzun (1885 – 1946) was a well-known writer and educationist, who published many essays, stories and translations.

About the essay: This essay was first published in *Middle School Students*, Issue 1, 1930. It is in a sarcastic tone that Xia Mianzun reveals some eating habits of the Chinese people.

Food and Other Things in Fuzhou

Yu Dafu

The food in Fuzhou, the capital city of Fujian Province, has been greatly appreciated by people of other places. About a dozen years ago, when mentioning family cooks in Beijing, we unanimously spoke highly of the dishes cooked by the chefs once hired by Mr. Liu Songsheng and Mr. Lin Zongmeng. The owner of a then very popular restaurant called Loyalty and Fidelity, which was located outside of the Xuanwu Gate, was just the former chef of the Liu Family, who had once worked in the imperial kitchen. The eating houses called The Small Youtian and the now closed Idle Villa in Shanghai had also been popular before Cantonese food took over the whole city. A kind of very delicious food called Yifu noodles is said to be the creation of Yi Moqing, an official of Tingzhou, who had also lived in Yangzhou for some years and had been in close contact with Yuan Zicai. It is a pity that he was not as considerate as the old man Sui Yuan, who had written a book of recipes and left it to us later generations; or he would be a Savarin of Fujian, known at home and abroad.

The Fujian food is famous for its richness, partly because of Fujian Province's rich natural resources. Fujian has coastal areas in the southeast and mountainous districts in the northwest. Delicacies from mountains and sea are plentiful and cheap. It is said that there has never been a need for the inhabitants along the coast to worry about the possibilities of going hungry. Just to walk along the seashore for some time after the ebb, one can pick up a basketful of marine products to eat. The warm land surface and fertile soil are good for trees and vegetable; one can plant and gather at any time all the year round. Not only can various vegetables be found and enjoyed in all the four seasons, but also edible wild herbs taste more delicious than those growing elsewhere. With the rich natural resources and a multitude of traveling officials and businessmen coming from other provinces, dishes in Fujian are usually made with ingredients taken from local places but cooked with various outlandish recipes. It is these unique combinations that make Fujian dishes the favorites of the gluttons. It should also be for this, that quite a number of writings were devoted to food in the two-volume book *Sketches on Fujian* by the Qing Dynasty scholar Zhou Lianggong.

Among all kinds of seafood in Fuzhou, clams from Changle and oysters from along the seashore are the most popular and delicious, especially during February and March. It is very likely that the "Xishi tongue" described as white, fleshy, crisp and fresh in *Sketches on Fujian* refers to the clam, which is regarded as ambrosia of good color, taste and scent if boiled with chicken soup. A story is circulating that the old and sick mother of the Secretary of the Navy wanted very much to have one more taste of clams, the delicacy of her native place. The son arranged an immediate airlift of clams to the capital and fulfilled his mother's last wish. This anecdote now serves as a sort of evidence for the distinctive flavor of clams. When I come to Fuzhou this time, clams are just in season. I have eaten hundreds of them, boiled or braised in brown sauce, and made myself a great glutton.

The oyster is by no means the special local product of Fuzhou, but Fujian's oysters are more fleshy, tender and pure than those caught elsewhere, such as in Jiangsu and Zhejiang Provinces. During the second and the third lunar months, stalls on the streets are piled with the light-blue watery meat of oysters, cheap but very tasty. They must be much more delicious than those Su Dongpo, the famous scholar of the Song Dynasty, ate in Lingnan, a vast area to the southwest of Fujian. What a pity it was that Mr. Su did not condescend to live in the coastal area of Fujian, otherwise he might not have bought the good farm land in Yangxian County, Jiangsu Province, but lived for generations at the foot of the three mountains and the two towers of Fuzhou. People in Fuzhou call the oyster as "diyi", which really need a proper Chinese word when writing down.

At the beginning of the Qing Dynasty, scallop was not as popular as now, hence Zhou Lianggong appreciated it very much and regarded it as a luxury. Today in Fuzhou, this kind of thing has already fallen into oblivion. Instead, the indispensable dish in a high-quality feast is a kind of crab, similar to the type commonly seen in Ningbo, which is called "Xin'en" by the Fuzhou people. It might be what is recorded as "tiger crab" in *Sketches on Fujian*. According to the Fuzhou people, meat from this kind of crab is very nourishing and easily digestible and hence the favorite of the sick, weak people and the lying-in women. But I have never favored any kind of crab, which I find rougher and less savory than clam or oyster or snail; I still agree with Zhou Lianggong's remarks on clam.

There are many other types of seafood besides the three mentioned above. However, the other types are commonly found elsewhere, and can often be tasted in Shanghai. It simply doesn't make sense to list them here.

As to the delicacies from the mountains, they can usually be dried and transported everywhere, so it is not necessary to talk about them either. The other thing that is worth mentioning is a queer kind of food wrapper called "meat swallow."

When I first came to Fuzhou, I toured the wide streets and narrow alleys and saw that in many shops there was a big chopping block in the middle, and on it one or two strong men were beating a large piece of pork with all their strength. I felt this was very strange and wondered why the pork was hit in this way. My Fuzhou friends explained that this would make the material for the "meat swallow," which is a kind of sheet made from the ground meat and wheat flour, just like the cover of *won ton*, used to wrap vegetables. As the final products— vegetables wrapped in this kind of cover look like swallows, hence the name. It is said that this is a unique creation of Fuzhou city and does not even belong to the province.

Fuzhou cuisine usually tastes sweet. The chicken and duck cooked by real Fuzhou restaurants are as sweet as candied fruit without the least touch of salt. Naturally, nine out of ten of Fuzhou people have decayed teeth. Once I went to a theatre in Fuzhou to watch the local opera and found that every actor or actress on the stage had a mouthful of golden teeth. When I turned to the audience on the left and right, I saw that most of them, men and women, also had golden teeth. Surrounded by people with the shining golden teeth, I, a monomaniac who has always hated golden teeth, was almost on the verge of tears, feeling that the Fuzhou people deliberately set out to make me suffer.

Compared with the sugary food, the yellowish-brown wine in Fuzhou is more enjoyable. Although I did not have a taste the various types of good wine described by Zhou Lianggong, such as Yudaichun (spring jade

41

tape）, Lihuabai（white pear flower）, Lanjia wine（blue family wine）, Bixia wine（green glow wine）, Lianxubai（white lotus stamen）Heqing（clear river）, Shuangjia, Xishi red wine（Xishi was a well-known beauty in ancient China—the translator）, Zhuangyuan red wine（state exam winner red wine）, etc. and can not make any comment on them, I did find everywhere a special kind of wine called "chicken wine", which was as red as amber and tasted a little bitter, and would cause a headache if one drank too much. According to the local people, the special effect and color of this wine are achieved by hanging an uncooked chicken in a sealed jar full of wine till all its meat and bones are dissolved. Then the jar can be uncovered and the wine is finally ready and enjoyed. Like other kinds of wine, it is better when preserved longer. The wine shops in Fuzhou are usually marked with the words "wine storehouse" outside and the selling of wine is called "carrying." These names sound rather original, if not strange in the trade since different dialects have different choices of words. The sweet wine made with red grains tastes like the sweet white spirit in Shanghai. Only its color is dark pink, which must have inspired such name as "Xishi Red" since its beautiful color reminds people of the famous ancient beauty Xishi. The litchi wine of Putian county is dark red and tastes like Bordeaux. However, I don't like this kind of wine though it is famous and costly. In Fuzhou, the wine served in banquets is usually a kind of high-grade Shaoxing wine—Huadiao, which is very costly and is always sold short weight. Moreover, its flavor is weaker than that in Shanghai and Hangzhou. For me, wine in Fujian is, after all, not as good as wine in Beijing.

Fruit, flowers and green trees can be seen in Fuzhou all the year round. Its oranges, tangerines, fingered-citron, litchi, longan, sugarcane, banana, jasmine, orchid, and olive are famous nation-wide. Since men of letters have already written a lot about them, here I can just save the trouble of mentioning them again.

Half of the tea in Fujian comes from Wuyi Mountain, but the people of the province usually like to crown all their tea with the name of the famous mountain. The two well-known types of Fujian tea, Iron Bodhisattva and Iron Arhat, both belonging to oolong tea, are regarded as the "rare type" among all kinds of tea. They are neither black nor green, but appear a little brown. If one is drunk, two or three cups of either type can really sober him up. The other types of Fujian tea are also exquisitely made and named. Not well versed in the knowledge of tea, I'm probably too vulgar to give appropriate comments on them, so I have to drop this subject here.

According to *Sketches on Fujian*, the sweet potato had been introduced by the Fujian people from southeast Asia as a sort of substitute for grains. Owing to its good taste and convenient way of planting, it later spread widely to the inland. The time of its introduction was traced back to three hundred years by Zhou Lianggong, to the turn of the Ming Dynasty and the Qing Dynasty. Although I don't know whether the time is exact or not, Fujian does have a history of lacking wheat and rice. Even now, Fujian still depends a great deal on other provinces or Taiwan for grains in spite of the fact that paddy can be planted and harvested twice a year. As a result, feasts in Fujian are mainly composed of dishes of all kinds, such as seafood, chicken, duck, pork, and vegetables, which will well fill the stomachs of those present before they help themselves to anything made of grains.

The famous restaurants within Fuzhou city are Spring Garden of Trees, The South Room, The Wine House on the River, The Good Pavilion, and so on. The Tasty Eating Place serves tasty and economic food, too. Moreover, the duck noodles at Cangqian, the vegetable dishes and beef served at Nanmendou, and the dumplings of the eating house to the west of the Drum Tower, all have a distinctive flavor. Even if you might not want to eat any of them too often, an occasional visit will satisfy you greatly. At the South Terrace outside the city there are several restaurants serving Western-style food: Building for All Guests, The Terrace for Western Feasts, The Grand French Restaurant, The Western Restaurant, and The Big Gathering Building, which faces the Minjiang River and includes a stage for performances. The Yixin Building beside the Hongshan Bridge is famous for its special dishes of some flatfish. The Merry Forest in Cangqianshan is good at choicely Western meat, fish and vegetable dishes. As to the dining room of the Youth Association where I lodge, it is a clean and spacious hall and serves both Chinese and Western food. But, unlike the Upper Room where Jesus entertained his twelve disciples freely, wine is forbidden in this dining room. Hence it is not good for formal dinner parties.

Fuzhou also possesses some unique hot-spring bathing places, such as the Lily Spring, the Dragon Spring outside the Tangmen Gate and the Happy Heaven Spring at the airport. These places all serve food and drink just for the convenience of the customers, who can spend the whole day there without going out to eat and drink. It is said that some time before, there were private pools for men and women to bathe together and eat together.

Before talking about the women of Fuzhou, the ethnical origin of the Fujian people should be examined. The earliest inhabitants of Fujian perhaps belonged to the ethnical group found on the islands near southeast Asia. People of this race somehow resembled the Japanese around Kyushu in features and customs. Later in the Spring and Autumn Period (770 – 496 BC), the Han people came down south and intermarried with the aboriginals and the race was thereafter called Wuzhu. Then in the Tang Dynasty (618 – 907 AD), a large number of troops arrived and, according to the legend, killed all the male Fujian inhabitants and left only women and girls to marry the bachelors in the army. Even today, the Fuzhou women still call their husbands "Tangbu People," that is, the Tang people who arrived in the evening. At the same time, women in Fuzhou are usually called "Zhu women," named after Wuzhu. The working women outside of the east gate and the north gate still wear the three knife-like silver hairpins, which are said to have been made as weapons to revenge their fathers, husbands or sons who were killed by the conquerors. Nowadays the prostitutes of Fujian origin in Taiwan still refuse to sleep with Japanese men though the conquest took place many, many years ago. If one of them dares make an exception and accept a Japanese man for a night, the others will all regard her as a beast in human clothing and break with her ever after. What a moving and tragic intolerance it is! Who said "singing among flowers of the back garden, the business women never know the rise and fall of the country?" Even the prostitutes are much loftier in this aspect than those who are betraying their country. The intermarriage between the Tang people and this ancient ethnical group did not take place completely. Some of the aboriginals now called the She nationality have continued their customs and religious rites and at present live a life of seclusion in the mountains outside of the north gate. Another nationality, said to be of Mongolian origin, usually lives on the water and has been regarded as lowly and often bullied by the Han people since the Ming and Qing Dynasties. It is said that these people were depreciated and were called Keti after the downfall of the Yuan Dynasty. Keti is actually a mispronunciation of Quti, which refers to these people's habit of sitting with bent knees in the cabins of their boats. Those who were called Quanlang in Quanzhou during ancient times, now colluded with the Japanese pirates and harassed the inhabitants along the coast just belong to a collateral branch of this people.

Owing to their mixed blood lineage and unique evolution as mentioned in the previous paragraph, the features of Fujian people are somehow different from those of the pure Han people in the Central Plains. The Fujian women usually have broad foreheads, deep eyes, high noses, prominent cheek bones, sunken cheeks and protruding jaws. It may be relatively common for men to have such features, but the women, with the distinctive features covered by smooth, white and delicate skin, look like the sharply contoured statues of human figures in ancient Greece. All Fuzhou women have excessively fair and fine skin. While this is natural for the girls who were born and bred in some officials' families and seldom go out, it is somewhat strange that the working women outside the city also have fair, rosy and delicate faces as if they have just made themselves up. Maybe the hot springs and the water of the Minjiang River make some contribution to their fine skin.

Not having lived in Fujian before, we had thought the Fujian people as a barbarous race. When we did arrive there and meet their culture, we began to realize that although they were late in becoming civilized, they had progressed and developed more quickly. Thanks to its coastal position and port cities, the province has much more frequent contact and cultural exchange with the Western countries than the remote inland areas. Some cities in southern Fujian are almost as prosperous and modern as Shanghai. With closer observation, you'll find women of Fujian are several times prettier than those of Shanghai and Hangzhou, and their health better and their dresses and ornaments are many times more stylish and fashionable than those of the small-sized Suzhou women.

As the ancient poem says: "A born beauty would find it hard not to display herself"; women usually have an instinct for decorating and exhibiting themselves. This instinct in Fuzhou women seems even stronger than that of women elsewhere. Whenever there is a fine day or a festival occasion, the south street and Cangqianshan will be full of pretty women: each has bright, dark eyes, high and narrow nose bridges, soft, white, delicate and smooth skin and each wears the most fashionable clothes and ornaments and make-up from Paris or New York. Who can pass unmoved by this beautiful and charming Fuzhou panorama in a fine day afternoon?

The instinct or fondness for fashion has also affected the society and the customs. As bankruptcy is a nation-wide economic fact and the girls and women mostly belong to an unproductive class below the middle level, it is only natural that lack of food and clothes will finally cause degradation of morals. A few months' stay in Fuzhou is long enough to hear that prostitution is rampant there. This is really a serious social problem, which, though unavoidable, requires immediate consideration and solution.

With the problem of prostitution already touched on, it is necessary to say a few words about the licensed prostitutes. In the past, Zhang Hengfu, a poet in Shaowu, wrote *Women of Nanpu*, a book devoted exclusively to records of romantic affairs of the prostitutes in the South Terrace of Fuzhou. Today with the depression, the brothels there have greatly declined, and no trace of the former prosperity and luxury can be found. The upper-class prostitutes in Fuzhou are very similar to those in Shanghai. But according to some friends who have long stayed in Fuzhou, they have few customers and live in poverty nowadays. Only the women who claim to merely sell their songs but not their bodies manage to keep the business: anyone who is willing to pay three *yuan* can be allowed to come in and listen to three operas. However, this business has also much declined; the once thriving singing houses have closed down one by one, leaving only three or five such houses in Tiandun. Apart from those mentioned above, there are outrageous and inhuman low prostitutes and secret traders in this occupation. The enormous number of these people and their eagerness to sell themselves are really appalling! As to the unlicensed prostitutes, the women that serve customers by month, and the retail places for this purpose, we have only heard say of some from the public security men or read about in newspapers. Though all their activities cannot be investigated, with the general economic slump and difficulty all over the country and the surplus of the population, one can well imagine what they might be up to.

In short, though people in Fuzhou may eat more extravagantly than people elsewhere, the social state of Fuzhou is not much more degenerate than other places. Their indulgence in sex and other desires is obviously related to the climate and local conditions. It is only natural that people in the subtropical zone have a greater need in these aspects than those in the frigid zone. The most unexpected things one finds, when coming to Fujian for the first time, are the great variety of food and the pretty and healthy women.

The translator's notes:

About the author: Yu Dafu (1896 – 1945) was a notable novelist and essayist. He also published translations and poems.

About the essay: This essay was first published in *Yijing*, Issue 9, July 5, 1936. Apart from some anthropological discussion of the origins of the Fujian people, he focuses on aspects of the popular culture in Fuzhou in the 1930s.

My Mother

Zou Taofen

To talk about my mother, I only know she was born in Haining County, Zhejiang Province and had a family name of "Cha," but I've never come to know her own name. This small incident reveals the difference between the old era and the present time. Nowadays, not only the unmarried girls dare to make their names known to the public "bravely," but also the married women are no longer shrinking from giving their full names. Not long ago, a married woman had to add her husband's family name to her own name, thus making the usual three-character name become a four-character name. When I was a child, I heard of a woman called Zhu-hu Binxia who wrote for *The Women's Journal* issued by The Commercial Press. She was at that time regarded as a revolutionary "progressive" woman, for she disagreed with the marriage forced on her by her family. Though threatened by her stubbornly conservative uncle to kill her with a pistol, she insisted on adding "Zhu," her family name, before "Hu," the family name of the man she was supposed to marry. Most recently, many married women still use their maiden names, without adding or omitting anything. This means that women have gradually come to obtain an independent status and are no longer the possession of anyone else. However,

50

in my mother's time, women seemed to have no names, to say nothing of inventing the name "Zhu-hu Binxia." Here, I use "seemed" because women at that time were not really nameless, the problem was that they simply could not find any use for their names. In the case of my mother, she was called "Miss Number 16" in her parents' family and then "Mistress Number 14" at her husband's home. Later, when my father secured an official position, she was called Madam. She just never got a chance to use her own name! I think all this serves as an implication of women's position in the feudal society of China.

My mother died when I was thirteen, according to the traditional method of counting age, which usually made one a year older than he actually was. In fact, I was born in September and my mother died in May, so we only lived together for about eleven years and nine months. The fragmentary recollections of my mother in this writing are only some glimpses of the happenings during those eleven years.

As far as I can remember, I had my first impression of Mother at the age of two or three. One evening, I was alone on the bed sleeping. I woke from a dream and opened my eyes drowsily. In the haziness I saw the faint lamp light coming through the bed curtain. Then a young woman opened the curtain and smilingly carried me in her arms. What she called me and said to me have already escaped me, I only remember she put me on her back and entered a large parlor which was brightly illuminated and crowded with people. It must have been the Lantern Festival, for except the adults talking and laughing, there were two or three dozen children running here and there in groups of three or five with colorful lanterns, all having small candles lighted inside. My mother walked around the parlor and I, prostrate on her back, still drowsy, looked at this or that with half-opened eyes. At that time, my father, as one of the young masters of the house, still lived with grandpa. My father had more than a dozen brothers, among whom several were already married, hence the dozens of children in the household. My mother, about 17 or 18 that year, had married into this large family by 15, and had given birth to me at 16. Even now when I recall my impression of her at the time when I was on her back, I can still feel her lively, cheerful, tender youth and beauty. Among all the women I have seen in my life, the most beautiful one is my mother. Even at the time when I was on her back, I could see that none of the women in the spacious parlor could match my mother in loveliness. Now with further thinking, I believe that it must have been the enthusiastic children with their lanterns that roused my mother's impulse to bring me out of the room to see the family carnival. She must have looked at me several times before I finally awoke. This is my first sensation of motherly love, though I was still too young then to have any idea of what was motherly love.

Some time later, my grandpa retired from office. My father brought his family to Fuzhou to be a candidate for an office vacancy. I was then about five or six years old and had a brother two years younger than I. The other member of the family apart from my parents and my brother was a girl servant called Little Sister, who came with mother as part of her marriage dowry. "Being an official" seemed to be a good thing, but my father, who had left his native place empty-handed, could do nothing but leave us in utter destitution. I remember that Father was seldom seen at home—maybe too busy with his social intercourse in the official circles. Sometimes, we had not even a grain of rice to cook. Little Sister would go to a nearby temple to get the charity rice for the poor. This involved pushing a way in a sea of people to obtain a bamboo slip. After that she had to squeeze in another huge crowd with the slip and a home-made cloth bag in her hand to get the rice. Meanwhile, my mother would hold my crying brother and walk to and fro at home. I used to sit on a small chair and stare at my mother blankly. Not knowing that this was what was called poverty, I wondered why my mother looked so pale. Her silence seemed indicative of some unspeakable load on her mind. Mother was on very intimate terms with Little Sister. They got along like mother and daughter, going through thick and thin together. Especially at the time when Mother was on the sickbed and very close to death, Little Sister simply took the place of a faithful daughter and tended Mother day and night, often forgetting to take her own meals and sleep.

Mother was fond of reading novels. She often told Little Sister of the stories she had read. She spoke with absorbing interest and Little Sister listened attentively, now smiling, now frowning. Some traditional Chinese novels had very long chapters which could not be finished in one sitting, and Little Sister would be very impatient to wait for Mother to read more and tell more. Sometimes, Mother's description of a single woman undergoing trials and tribulations or the wrong done to a righteous woman would reduce them both to tears. At such times, I would stand aside looking on, making neither heads nor tails of why they were crying. Not until now have I begun to see my mother as a woman of rich emotions. Since she could tell a story in such a way that deeply moved Little Sister, she would have been able to make herself a very skilled teacher if she could have lived till now.

My father started my education in person with a volume of *Three-character Songs* when I was six years old. In the first class, I was taught to read the following:

At birth, men are good.

Similar in nature, different in habits.

Sitting on the *kang* (bed made of brick or mud brick in China—the translator) in a small parlor, I read these words aloud over and over again without the meaning of them sinking in. What a painful effort it was! My mother insisted on getting a formal teacher in case I would be led astray. So she decided to economize further on the already stinting food and clothing in order to save enough money to hire a teacher. It might sound unbelievably cheap since the first teacher cost us only four silver dollars a month apart from free board and lodging. Yet, such a small sum still took all my mother's efforts to collect. When I was ten, I began to read "The Interview between Mencius and Emperor Liang Hui." By then the teacher's salary had been raised to twelve silver dollars a month, three times of that at the beginning. At the end of the year, my father wanted to examine all the schoolwork I had done. He sternly let me recite one text after another at night and put a bamboo slab of more than one inch wide on the table. I stood with my back facing him and began the recital. Whenever there was a pause or a word needed to be prompted, he would ask me to turn around and lay my hand on the table. Then he would severely hit the palm of my hand with the bamboo slab. The pain was so great that I could not help crying. But I had to hold back my tears and turned around to recite again. Unfortunately, I paused once more and had another word prompted, so I got another hit on the palm, and was sobbing through "The Interview between Mencius and Emperor Liang Hui." The sound of sobbing must have stirred my mother very much, for the sound of suppressed weeping was heard from where my mother was sitting with her needlework. I understood she was painfully sympathetic with me when I was hit. Yet, in order that I could draw some lessons from the hits and make more progress, she had to give her assent to the punishment with the words: "Well done," which were actually squeezed between her bursts of weeping. The forced "well done" revealed the complicated feelings of the maternal love and urging. Although it seems to me now this is a very savage way of education, I cannot lay the blame on my mother. Savage as it is, it was the only way available at that time. Besides, my mother's love towards me, shown through all her sobs and weeping, has always made me recall her with gratitude. The moment I finished reciting half the volume on Emperor Liang Hui, my right hand swelled more than half an inch high. I put my hand in the light of the lamp stealthily and found the bloated palm almost shining, just like the body of a silkworm about to spin silk. Later, still in tears, my mother put me to bed. She covered me with the quilt and then kissed me on the forehead.

At the time I was eight, my brother was six and my sister was three. Mother made for us all the clothes, shoes and socks we needed. Moreover, she often took in some needlework to help support the family. The sewing always kept her very busy. I was already old enough to feel upset when seeing Mother working hard. I remember one summer night I woke up from a dream and found Mother sitting alone by the light, stitching a shoe sole. Being much stirred by Mother's toil, I turned over in bed and was unable to fall asleep again. I wanted to get up to keep my mother company. Knowing that I would be scolded for not sleeping late at night even if I had a very good reason, I tried another excuse. I called Mother and told her I felt too hot to sleep and wanted to sit for a while to get cooled. Rather unexpectedly, I was allowed to sit beside her. I felt disturbed to see the beads of sweat streaming down from her forehead, but she herself seemed to be unaware of this and put one stitch after another into the sole—she was making cloth shoes for me. At this hour of the night, all was quiet. I could only hear the tick of the clock and the breath of my mother. A kind of guilty feeling suddenly came upon me—it was for me that my mother toiled so late. Sitting beside Mother to keep her company made me feel a little better. However, I did not dare tell Mother what was really on my mind. After a while, my mother asked me to go back to bed with the words: "As a child, why not have a good sleep on bed but get up at midnight!" Now my mother has passed away, she did not and will never know this untold state of mind of her son on that particular night.

Mother died at the age of twenty-nine, leaving behind her three sons and three daughters. The night before her death, she remained fully conscious and with tears called her children one by one, exhorting us for the last time. Among all the things in the world, it was her children that she felt most unwilling to part with.

On the whole, my mother was just an ordinary mother. But I think if her lovable character, her capacity and exertion had not been stifled in a feudal family and wasted on household trifles, she would have contributed more to the society. Who knows how many women like my mother have been stifled and ruined!

The translator's notes:

About the author: Zou Taofen (1895 – 1944) was a well-known journalist, political commentator and publisher.

About the essay: This essay was written in January, 1936, referring to the feudal family, traditional education and women's status and life at the turn of the 19th century and 20th century in China. The translation is based on the original essay that is included in *Writings by Taofen* published in 1955.

Part Ⅱ

Concern About the Old Man Under the Moon

Ye Zhishan

Once upon a time there was a temple for the old man under the moon—the god who unites persons in marriage—beside the West Lake. I went there once when I was small, yet I cannot remember everything clearly since fifty-five years have passed. I believe that on the east bank of the West Lake stood the White Cloud Nunnery, and the temple for the old man under the moon was just on the left side of the nunnery, but since both have vanished, there is no need to be elaborate on the exact locations of them. The temple, which seemed little known then, was very quiet. It had only a small courtyard and three or five tile-roofed rooms. No tea was served and there was no one to collect the incense money. In the middle of the principal room was a shrine, in which sat the Marriage-uniting God. The god was an old man with a thick white beard, and pinkish face, who wore a red cowl-like hat and a red cloak, very similar to an old landlord in the traditional dramas, and the god was painted to smile brightly. On the altar in front of the shrine were set an incense burner, a candlestick and a container holding bamboo slips used for drawing lots. Below on the ground was the rush cushion one usually expected of such a place. An antithetical couplet on black lacquer boards was found on both sides of the shrine. It was written in the old man's tone:

May the lovers in the world become couples;

Miss no opportunity of marriage that is destined.

The couplet had no punctuation marks; it was I who added them to it. Later I learned that the first line had been taken from a classic Chinese novel on love—*The Story of the West Wing-room*. In any case, the old man's noble ambition reflected in the line was really moving and respectable. The second line of the couplet seemed contradictory—how could the destined be missed? If they could be missed, then what was the sense of talking about "destined?" Upon further consideration, I saw the second line was connected with the first. It was the intention of the old man, who wished for the best and was trying to warn young people not to be fanciful and fickle in love affairs. I should have understood that there was little logic in this sort of encouragement to marry.

When I visited the temple of the Marriage-uniting God, I was merely twelve years old. It was autumn, just the time for drinking the special chestnut and osmanthus flower soup according to the traditional custom. The whole family, my grandma, father, mother, sister, brother and I, six people of three generations, went together. We stayed in Hangzhou for six days, half of which was spent on the lake. One day, my grandma hired a rickshaw and went alone as a pilgrim to Tian Zhu Mount on the west side of the lake. It was decided beforehand that the driver of the rickshaw should take care of her in time of need during the trip. Meanwhile, my parents took us children to go sightseeing on the West Lake in a small rowboat. When we reached the Sudi Dyke, Father asked the boatman if he knew the temple for the god who unites people in marriage. With a nod the boatman let the rowboat pass through one of the bridge openings of the dyke and rowed forward along the reedy bank. My parents told us that they had traveled to Hangzhou and visited this very temple when they had just married. Then they talked of the well-known antithetical couplet and of the story behind it: it was said there had been a poor scholar who once lodged in the temple, reading books every day. He was so poor that he could not even pay for his meals, so he had to make a living by selling his calligraphy. The couplet was his creation, and he also made a set of lot-drawing slips for the god. The whole set was composed of one hundred slips, each bearing an extract from the classics. My mother said that last time she happened to draw a slip which had the words taken from *The Book of Songs*, which read as follows: "Bears make an auspicious sign of a coming man". Sure enough, later, I, a man, was born. On hearing this, I grew very interested in the temple. As soon as we disembarked, I ran into the principle room before all the others and drew a bamboo slip from the container. As luck would have it, on the slip was written: the first lot, the most auspicious. To get the label for the lot, one should pay about a dozen copper coins. Yet, instead of finding someone from whom I could buy the label, I saw the labels all hanging on the back wooden partition of the shrine. I tore the label for the first lot and found it bearing the opening words of *The Book of Songs*: "The aquatic birds are chirping on the banks of the river; the gentle, graceful and fair maidens are what the gentlemen court". At that time I had only a hazy notion of what these lines meant, but I knew that one thing was certain—I would have no trouble finding a wife since it was "destined. "

Maybe the old man under the moon indeed helped me cryptically, for I married the girl I loved without a hitch. I felt I was obliged to report this to the old man. However, when I went to Hangzhou again to revisit this

god with good intentions for human beings after the War of Resistance A-
gainst Japan, I saw only withered grass and a scene of desolation where the
temple had stood.

    With this recollection finished, I will make a suggestion. As the his-
toric sites around the West Lake have one after another been renovated, the
temple of the old man under the moon, though not a typical historic site,
deserves to be rebuilt as well. It will not cost much to build a few tile-
roofed rooms and a small courtyard and to mold a statue of the old man.
Since many young couples come to the West Lake to spend their leisure
time together, it would clearly be a good thing to set up this additional temple that is relevant to their real concern during this special period of life,
and where they can confide to the old man what they think and want. An
antithetical couplet would also be needed. The first line of the former couplet should be retained, but the second line sounds a little fatalistic. If it
can be replaced by a better one, that will be fine; but if no suitable substi-
tution can be found, we'd better leave it alone. It's often the case that some
amusing thing may have a touch of superstition, yet if you refuse to view it
superstitiously, then amusement will be all left in it. The other necessary
things are the container for holding the bamboo slips and the labels for
lots. To write good wishes on the labels and make the young couples who
are passionately in love happy can be a meritorious deed. Only the abstruse
and archaic words and expressions should not be followed when writing the
labels.

    The translator's notes:

About the author: Ye Zhishan (1918 – 2006) was a well-known writer and senior editor, whose major works are two collections of literary writ-

ings co-authored with Ye Zhimei and Ye Zhicheng.

About the essay: This essay was written on May 22, 1985 and then published in *Zhejiang Pictorial*, Issue 12, 1985. At that time, people began to reexamine the Cultural Revolution (1966 – 1976), which regarded a lot of Chinese traditions as feudal dregs. It is against this background that the author expressed his nostalgic feeling towards some of the Chinese traditions.

The Dragon Boat Festival

Chen Baichen

I loved the Dragon Boat Festival.

The Dragon Boat Festival was also called the Fifth Day Festival, the Cattail Festival, and in my hometown the Fifth Lunar Month Festival.

I liked the Dragon Boat Festival not for the vacation from school, as the holiday only lasted a day or half a day, but I liked it for the day's events.

The customs are not confined to dragon boat racing only, but include many other activities. On this day, every family would hang some cattail and Chinese mugwort on the front door and a portrait of the God of Judgment on the wall. The typical mid-day meal of the festival was composed of realgar wine and *zongzi*, a pyramid-shaped dumpling made of glutinous rice wrapped in bamboo or reed leaves. Children would wear tiger-shaped shoes, and in addition, girls would be given a string of ornaments each to hang on their chest and boys would have the Chinese character "王" meaning "the king" written with realgar on their forehead. These were precautions against the five poisonous creatures—scorpion, viper, centipede, house lizard and toad. The leaves of the Chinese mugwort would be burned in order to produce a strong fragrant scent to drive away evil spirits. At mid-day, the variety of traditional Dragon Boat Festival activities would be brought into full play, and shops in the entire town were all closed for the occasion. During the Festival, even the people who were in debt would feel free to appear in public and their creditors would have no right to ask for payment. Shortly after noon, when people finished the festival dinner and felt a little drunk with the realgar wine, they would go out to watch the dragon boat racing in their best—or at least more presentable—clothes.

I'm not a person who ever really studied customs, but generally customs reflect the history and culture of a nation. The Dragon Boat Festival, though I cannot tell when it started, seemed to comprise two things. First, it had been started to the memory of Qu Yuan, the first greatest poet of ancient China, who plunged into a river and drowned on the fifth day of the fifth lunar month as a protest against the fatuous ruler of his kingdom. The dragon boat racing was a ceremony to lament his death, and *zongzi*, the dumpling specially made to throw into the river, was a sacrificial offering for the soul rested in it.

Second, as I've mentioned, the Dragon Boat Festival was a day meant for avoidance of harmful creatures or evil spirits. In fact, it had become a day for hygiene and health, for there was a scientific touch behind its superstitions. However, we have often made the mistake of simply regarding these customs as utterly superstitions and opposing them without the least study of them. This is not a scientific attitude. The Japanese have seemed to be more enlightened than us in this aspect. Though they were much Europeanized after the Meiji Reformation, they preserved more of their traditional customs than we kept those of ours. For example, they still wear the kimono and observe their traditional methods of drinking tea and raising flowers. Even the ancient Chinese dancing tune "The Lanling King entering the Array" and the Tang music now already lost in China have still been kept in Japan owing to its practice of keeping its customs intact.

Now let's return to the festival from the digression about Japan. Although whether hanging a stalk of cattail on the door can avoid evil spirits still requires more research before verification, the hanging of the leaves of mugwort, a kind of traditional Chinese medicine, is really reasonable. One evidence of this is that the Chinese acupuncture and moxibustion has already entered the international medical circle and the moxa used in this treatment is just made of mugwort. When I was small, I used to offer the sacrifice to Zhong Kui, the God of Judgment, with the leaves of mugwort burning, filling the room with a fragrant scent.

If we change its so-called purpose of avoiding the evil spirits into that of getting rid of flies and mosquitoes, isn't it a good method for hygiene? People in the countryside often make cord by twisting the moxa and then burn the cord to drive away flies and mosquitoes. As for realgar, it is a kind of medicine recorded in *Compendium of Materia Medica* (the book on Chinese herbal medicine), which can be used for detoxication and as insecticide, and applied externally will cure mange, scab and snake or insect bites. People's drinking the realgar wine at the festival is taking the medicine orally and their writing the character on the forehead is just the external application. Both are good for prevention of the five poisonous creatures; clearly there is more in the custom than mere superstition.

The act of hanging the portrait of Zhong Kui and offering a sacrifice to him can be regarded as superstitious, but as it was said that Zhong Kui could catch ghosts or spirits, the portrait of him was a sort of spiritual comfort for the common people at the period when science had not been developed. Of course, I've never believed in the legend about him. It says that the Tang emperor Xuanzong once had malaria and dreamed of a great spirit that caught and ate small ghosts and claimed to be the soul of a scholar who killed himself by bumping his head against the stairs after he failed the imperial examinations. This frightened the emperor so much that he got over the malaria. Hence the emperor ordered Wu Daozi to draw a picture of Zhong Kui and distributed copies of it to the officials. It seems ridiculous for Master Zhong to have such blind faith in examinations. If one has real ability and learning, why must he strive for a "degree?" As to the Tang emperor Xuanzong, his orders to have Zhong Kui's picture drawn and worshipped seem more extreme. For example, during the later period of the Cultural Revolution, a number of people committed suicide for their failure in examinations. Even if there had been hundreds of Wu Daozi, how could all of them be drawn and worshipped? It is also said that there was never any person called Zhong Kui, which was in fact a kind of plant, pronounced the same as Zhong Kui the god of Judgment, though written differently in Chinese. As the plant could be used to drive away spirits, people invented Zhong Kui the god according to its pronunciation. If the second story is true, then the function of Zhong Kui is just the same with that of realgar and leaves of mugwort—all for the prevention of diseases. However, with the establishment of any myth, the protagonist in it acquires great artistic force. To this day, we would rather have Zhong Kui, the God of Judgment, instead of believing in the story of the plant. I remember in my childhood, my family hung a portrait of Zhong Kui at every Dragon Boat Festival, though I never knew who had drawn the picture since it was clearly not the authentic work of Wu Daozi. I suspected that it might be my father's own drawing, but I did not venture to ask him about it. In fact, that portrait of Zhong Kui was fairly lovable, or rather, it looked more human than godlike. It is a great pity that it was lost long ago. Later, when I saw Zhong Kui appearing in many dramas and plays, I liked him even more. Even now, his seemingly ferocious but actually lovable face can still be seen in the classic dramas, say, *Zhong Kui Getting His Sister Married* and *Ms. Li Hui*. Immortal as he is, the pity remains that he has now been separated almost completely from the festival. Otherwise, isn't life more beautiful during the festival if the picture of Zhong Kui called "Dare the Ghost Come" drawn by Comrade Tian Yuan is hung at every home? However, when I talk of hanging the picture of Zhong Kui at every home, I excluded the homes of the young and middle-aged intellectuals, who are still waiting to get proper living quarters, not to mention a parlor where they can put up the picture of Zhong Kui.

When the sacrificial rites for the God of Judgment were over, the midday dinner was served. Once at the dinner table, I always tried to be the first to snatch the halved salted duck eggs coated with realgar. The eggs had been sunned in the courtyard at noon, though I could not find the reason why they should be sunned. The oily yolk of the salted egg, together with the realgar was delicious all the same. And then the family feast followed. For a comparatively well-off family like ours, we had two indispensable dishes—cold bean jelly dressed with sauce, and fried finless eel, in addition to many other dishes. The cold dish might serve to vindicate the arrival of the hot summer and the latter dish seemed to symbolize the conquest of the snake, one of the poisonous creatures. The homely-made fried eel, though not as good as that cooked in a restaurant, was actually very tasty when dressed with Chinese chives and pepper. With the two dishes as my favorites I paid so little attention to the other meat and fish dishes that I forget them all. Moreover, I usually ate as fast as I could in order to depart early after dinner for the dragon boat racing.

However, the adults were not in a hurry. Mother and my sisters-in-law had yet to deck themselves out, and Father and my brothers to be dressed in their best. Even I was given a long robe and mandarin jacket to wear! How disgusting it was! The long robe was basically made of silk, but the upper part was of grass cloth. We called this a "two-section robe." My second teacher Mr. Gu used to wear this kind of robe in summer. According to him, silk stuck to the skin when one sweated and cloth didn't, but actually it was a device for frugality. Anyhow when one put on the black gauze mandarin jacket, nobody could see the upper part of the robe. A ten-year-old boy like me, when dressed in the robe and jacket, looked very much like a young diehard of the Qing Dynasty, though without the night-stool-like cap and the pigtail at the back of my head. Unfortunately, I could not protest against the attire but slipped into it, for my mother often boasted about her great capacity for managing to get her children very decently patched even in the hardest days, to say nothing of the comfortable present days.

At last the whole family, men and women, set out, passed the east town gate and headed for the quay. Along the southern bank of the Dazhatang, there were several steamship companies, such as Zhaoshang, Taigu, Dai Shengchang, etc. As my father was a regular customer who often took a steamship to Zhejiang and Shanghai, he was given a place on the quay of Dai Shengchang or Zhaoshang. We all stood there to watch the festivities. To get a clearer view and to be more comfortable, one had to hire a boat and watch in the middle of the river. Yet only the officials, the gentry and the rich men could afford to or be allowed to. For us, we simply had no choice but to stand on our legs.

The dragon boat racing had long begun. There was a deafening sound of gongs and drums accompanied by cheers from time to time. On the decorated boats, each with a dragon head and tail, drummers waved the drumsticks very enthusiastically and the gong-beaters kept the gong ringing in the same zest, all striving to win the race! While watching, I managed to slip out of my jacket and robe one after the other.

The most wonderful performance was still to follow—the performance in the water by swimmers. I can remember at least three kinds of performance: first, to get and bite duck eggshells floating on the water; second, to chase after a duck; third, to recover coins thrown into the river water. The winner could collect prize money from the spectators.

I never could work out what the relationship was between the duck eggs and the Dragon Boat Festival, but there must be some reason for us to have had duck eggs at lunch and for the swimmers to compete to bite the duck eggshells in the water. It would require an anthropologist to give an answer. At any rate, the performance of catching the eggshells was exciting and entertaining. As soon as rich spectators threw them into the water, many swimmers began to chase the light and smooth eggshells. However, as they floated fast away with the flowing water, few swimmers could come near them. Even if one or two of the fastest swimmers was lucky enough to catch up with an eggshell, at the moment the swimmer opened his mouth to bite it, it slipped fast away. This competition would last a long time, and every try and miss would rouse loud acclamations or sighs from the people lining the riverbanks. When someone finally bit a shell, he would be thunderously hailed by all spectators on the two banks and duly rewarded.

According to some specialists, the performance of chasing after the duck was rather cruel. The top of the duck's head was cut open and quicksilver was placed right in the cut to make the pain extremely keen. Then the duck was put into the water and the great pain usually made it dive deeply. Yet the water would inevitably worsen the pain, and it would soon come to the surface again. The swimmers, at this time, would race to catch it from all directions, which would frighten the duck into a more desperate dash for life. It might even flee towards the upper reaches. To chase after it, the swimmers had to struggle ahead against the current and the whirlpools. This exertion was so breathtaking that the roaring cheers rose again. The hero who caught the duck in the end would hold his captive high in the water and later got a sum of prize money.

As for the coin recovery, it was less interesting than the other performances. The high-rank official or wealthy men on the boats in the river usually threw several silver dollars into the water and the swimmers would dive deep into the water to catch them with their mouths. When anyone succeeded in doing this, the silver dollar would be his. Not only was this game too simple, but also it seemed to be a display of wealth enjoyed only by the rich. I was rather disgusted with it. The other kinds of performance, though exciting, also had a profits-before-everything tendency. Isn't it better when a prize cup or gold medal is awarded to the winners like in today's sports activities?

Now, I'm having my seventy-sixth Dragon Boat Festival, but I find it only a lonesome festival. What a magnificent sight it would be if there were dozens or hundreds of dragon boats racing under the great bridge of the Yangtze River! Among the sports events, there is speedboat racing, but why not include dragon boat racing since this traditional sport can build up the people's health as well as enrich the recreational activities? It seems that at present this custom has only been observed in Guangtong Province and several minority nationality regions. Why is it so exclusive in such a vast country? In recent years, with the enrichment of the country people, many traditional folk recreational activities have been restored. For instance, swinging boats on the lake, performing the lion dance, walking on stilts and playing the dragon dance have begun to appear on the TV screens. It is a pity that though the dragon is said to be originally a creature living in water, it is now only allowed to dance on land.

This day is also the 2,262nd anniversary of Qu Yuan, yet, the lamentable thing is that commemorative activities have not been devoted to the great dead, but to someone who is still alive. I don't know how the Chinese poets will think about it. I remember during the Anti-Japanese War, the Chinese poets made this very day the festival for poets. It is strange that after the liberation in 1949, nobody has mentioned this any more. Perhaps once liberated, our poets no longer need the protection of this ancient poet? Or because they feel that his suicide made him a bad example?

I'm not a poet myself. I've written this recollection while biting at *zongzi*. Though I never felt lonesome on this day in my childhood, I feel extremely so when I put down my pen!

Written on the Dragon Boat Festival of 1984 in Nanjing.

Postscript: When I finished the above, I put it aside for a couple of days in case I wanted to correct some part of it. Meanwhile, quite unlike the previous years, news and pictures on the Dragon Boat Festival and the Poet Festival have appeared in newspapers and on TV screens. It is very inspiring to see the scenes of dragon boat racing in Hangzhou, the capital of Zhejiang Province and Chongqing, a city in Sichuan Province on TV and to hear the news about the dragon boat racing in Tongling, Anhui Province and Foshan, Guangtong Province. Only the race to compete for the "Qu Yuan Cup" in Foshan is to be held on September 16th. What a long time it is to wait! The great poet Qu Yuan has now been mentioned again and a-gain, and crowds of tourists, domestic and foreign, have visited the Tem-ple of Qu Yuan on the bank of Gu Luo River during the two days. News has also come from Shanghai that an international writing conference was held especially marked "for the Poet Festival in memory of the great Chi-nese poet Qu Yuan" to draw attention of foreign poets and writers, al-though it seems that few contemporary Chinese poets attended it. Moreo-ver, there was one or two other report meetings or lectures in memory of Qu Yuan and the Dragon Boat Festival. All these most recent activities consti-tute a comfort to me and make it necessary for me to add the above several sentences to what I wrote a few days ago to save the readers the trouble of correcting me. Still, my feeling of loneliness remains, though with some e-motions caused by the above added. May celebration of the traditional fes-tival and commemorative activities of Qu Yuan be held in the whole country instead of only in a few cities or areas, and among the masses as well as a-mong the poets. I will feel very happy if this can really happen and make the postscript together with my recollection become sheer nonsense!

The translator's notes:

About the author: Chen Baichen (1908 – 1994) was a professor, writer, playwright and drama theorist, who published three collections of essays and three plays.

About the essay: This is another essay that was written in mid – 1980s to call for restoration of the Chinese traditional customs, which was regarded as feudal dregs and fell into oblivion during the Cultural Revolution (1966 – 1976). The author not only expressed his nostalgic feelings towards the traditional Dragon Boat Festival, but also his strong wish that proper observation of this tradition should be restored nation-wide.

Tianyi Pavilion in the Winds and Rains

Yu Qiuyu

I

For some reason, I had always been separated from Tianyi Pavilion, an old traditional Chinese building storing a large collection of books. It should have been the privileged place for me, a scholar who loves books dearly. Besides, it is located in Ningbo, the very city where I was born. It might appear abnormal that I had never entered the pavilion that I should have visited frequently long ago. In the spring of 1976, I went to Ningbo for a rest at the house of my former teacher, Mr. Sheng Zhongjian, to regain my health after a serious disease. During my stay, Mr. Sheng tried to make arrangements for me to read for some time in Tianyi Pavilion. But at that time, to get this kind of permission, one had to go through very complicated formalities. Moreover, I was not in the mood to read, so we let the matter drop. Later, the atmosphere for academic study was improved and my friends in the cultural and artistic circles of Ningbo regularly invited me to give lectures. But every time I went and returned in a great hurry and never got a chance to visit Tianyi Pavilion.

With the recent fad of tourism, many ordinary Shanghai citizens who toured in Ningbo for a few days would come back talking of Tianyi Pavilion excitedly. This made it even more peculiar that I, though often studying the reprinted copies of the books kept at Tianyi Pavilion and knowing a great deal about the place's vicissitudes, had never been there. In August, 1990, I was invited again to Ningbo to give lectures. When I finished, I shyly asked my host, Mr. Pei Minghai, the deputy director of the cultural bureau, who took charge of Tianyi Pavilion, for a visit to the pavilion. After expressing great shock at the revelation that I had not been there yet, he decided to accompany me to Tianyi Pavilion the following day.

However, that very night the city was struck and shaken by a violent typhoon, followed by torrential rain. The next morning, when we arrived at the pavilion as arranged, we saw the entire courtyard flooded and fallen leaves swirling on the surface of the water. Even the brick walls looked wet and gloomy.

The old doorkeeper had never expected that the deputy director of the cultural bureau would take a visitor there in such bad weather. Hastily, he borrowed two pairs of knee-high rubber boots from the sanitation workers for us to wear and gave us two umbrellas. But the water in the courtyard was too deep for the boots; they were full of water as soon as we began to walk across the yard. We had to give up the boots and rolled up our trousers and walked barefoot in the water. We had already been chilled by the wind and rain; now, with our feet touching the water, each of us began to shiver all over. Supporting each other, we managed to waddle along towards the pavilion. How difficult it was for me to reach it! Even though I was near enough to it, the water, wind and rain together set up the last barrier between us. I knew that all through the history it had been difficult for scholars to enter the pavilion and read the books there. Perhaps all the hardship I met this day in order to come into the pavilion was just a ferocious ceremony presided over by God.

The person who established Tianyi Pavilion took from *Yijing—the Book on Changes* an expression, "tian yi sheng shui" meaning "if heaven delivers water," and adopted the first two characters of the original Chinese phrase as the name of building. As *Yijing—the Book on Changes* has been among the well-known classics, most Chinese people, especially the intellectuals, could easily see that this name, with its implication of water, indicated conquest of fire. This, he believed, would protect it forever from fire, a book collector's greatest worry. Now, when I came to Tianyi Pavilion for the first time, Heaven showed me all the implications of its name and made me "take part in" the ceremony with the most devout appearance: barefoot and obsequiously shivering, with no trace of the ease and gentleness possessed by a visitor in most cases. Moreover, there were no visitors apart from myself on this particular day. Wasn't all this an unusual arrangement?

II

Having undergone a lot of hardship and tragedies, Tianyi Pavilion as a book-storing building has actually become a cultural miracle.

As one of the ethnic groups that created the oldest civilizations in the world, the Chinese nation admirably invented the most unique and beautiful pictographic characters, the ancient books copied on bamboo and silk, and then in due course, invented paper and printing. All these inventions should have provoked a booming increase in book production and a rapid spread of Chinese civilization. However, what history saw was only the burning of the thin pages of books in the flames of savage wars and the engulfing of the fragile wisdom in endless ignorance. As a result, the nation that prepared all the conditions for book writing and printing could not dig-

77

nifiedly possess and preserve books. Books were somehow regarded as rare and strange things. The spiritual world of this nation was long in a state of confusion and spontaneity, the people often not knowing whence they came, or where they were going, or who they were, or what they should do.

Each wise man of the nation knew, of course, how important books were to the people. Only books could thread the events all through their long history, to produce a common culture among the numerous ethnic groups, and to preserve the seeds of civilization on such an immense land. Fortunately, there was a great number of scholars or men of letters who made it a profession of copying and keeping safe their books. Nevertheless, it was always very difficult for the usually impoverished scholars to collect considerable quantities of books and keep them intact for generations. According to the classics, "The bounties bestowed by a monarch may turn into the punishment of chopping off the head after five generations." Even scholarly honor, official rank, properties, good farmland and towering buildings could not last long, so how could a few boxes of books?

The imperial palace usually had some collection of books, but little could be expected of this since these ways of keeping books before the Qing Dynasty were not up to standard as far as their cultural significance was concerned. Moreover, books kept in the palace were often destroyed with dynastic changes. Owing to all of these factors, the task of preserving books was eventually entrusted to special persons, mainly long-term officials whose positions and work transfers allowed them to travel a lot, thus enabling them to collect editions available in various places. Additionally, they generally had reached a high cultural level and were sensitive to the value of books and, most practical in library management. That is to say, they should have shrewd considerations for library construction, bookcase design, reading regulations and fire-prevention measures. Furthermore, they should have far-reaching future plans, for preserving their collections of books from generation to generation. Only when a man had all the a-bove-mentioned qualifications could he become a book collector in ancient China.

There was indeed, in due time, a host of such collectors. But several generations later, their book-collecting cause came to a halt one after an-other. Though these still known collectors' names would make a long list, not one copy has survived from these early efforts. Consequently, these names simply stood for a kind of eventually fruitless effort, some tragic as-piration which had once been realized but was futile after a period.

Could there not be one more person, who was able to make more rig-orous the conditions mentioned above and conceive extremely strict meas-ures for storage management, conservation and inheritance of a book col-lection in order to be sure that China would have one place for a proper book repository? May God show mercy to China and the Chinese culture.

There at last appeared such a person—the founder of Tianyi Pavilion named Fan Qin.

Ruan Yuan, a scholar of the Qianjia period in the Qing Dynasty once said: "Tianyi Pavilion of the Fan family has lasted hundreds of years and remains as the only book-repository building in the country. "

The books recording the Chinese civilization collected during the sev-eral hundreds of years from the Ming Dynasty to the Qing Dynasty had fi-nally found a home.

Without mention of the long history before the Ming Dynasty, nor of the books that had not been collected, we should at least kowtow to this building for having sheltered our nation's cultural history, though sporadic and fragmentary.

III

Fan Qin lived in the Jiajing period of the Ming Dynasty. After he had passed the highest imperial examinations at the age of 27, he secured an official position and traveled all over China, such as to Shaanxi, Henan in the north, Guangdong, Guangxi, Yunnan in the south and Fujian, Jiangxi in the east. He was later promoted to vice-minister of the Ministry of War—a high-ranking post in feudal China. This provided him with the financial resources and mobility necessary for book collection. At a time when cultural data was difficult to gather owing to lack of such market, an official's position was itself an important license to collect books.

At every place to which his position brought him, Fan Qin would keep his eyes open in collecting the local block-printed editions made publicly or privately, including the local chronicles, the political books, records and data on tests, etc. usually neglected by or inaccessible to other book collectors.

Even some transient poetry anthologies printed by local officials were included in his collection. To accomplish all of this, mere possession of enthusiasm and financial resources was not enough. Seemingly he was amusing himself with book collecting; actually he regarded it as the most essential task in his life. In his heart, he put book collecting before anything else, including being an official, which he often used as a means to fulfill his life aim. This priority was in fact a historic decision. It seemed that history wanted a book collector in China at that particular time, and he was given the position whose traveling nature helped him to fill this need.

For him, all of the duties he had performed as vice-minister, such as trying an important case, impeaching a corrupt official, mediating a dispute between officials, or clearing some financial affairs, along with all of the dignity and fame brought to him by the high official's position, was nothing compared with the tiny cloth parcel presented to him by a runner in the evening, containing the old books he awaited. The rustling sound produced by a careful reader leafing through one of these books rang much louder in his mind than the gong beating and the loud cries to clear the way for his sedan when he went out.

Fan Qin's preference coincides with the topic I have been concerned with in recent years: intuitive cultural knowledge based on sound personality, or, conversely, sound personality based on intuitive cultural knowledge. Without this capacity, he could not have been so firm and persistent in his enterprise, slighting what was valued dearly by the common people and valuing dearly what was slighted by them. He once bluntly contradicted Guo Xun, a very powerful and influential relative of the emperor, and was therefore beaten in court and then put into prison. After his release, he was as honest and frank as ever, and later offended the Yan family— both the father and son being treacherous court officials of high rank. Yan Shifan, the son, wanted to take measures to discharge him from his post, but his father Yan Song held him back with the words: "Fan Qin is such a person who even dared to contradict Guo Xun! If you impeach him, you will only make him more famous. " So the Yan family had to leave him alone. From the aforementioned anecdotes we can see a successful book collector should at least be sound and strong in personality.

At this point, we may compare Fan Qin with the other book collectors of his own time. One of Fan Qin's friends, the master calligrapher, Feng

Fang, also collected books. As the first merit to be mentioned, his handwriting was undoubtedly better than what Fan Qin could ever accomplish, and his achievements in calligraphy were admirably acknowledged by Dong Qichang, the famous calligrapher, who entitled him one of the great masters of calligraphy of the Ming Dynasty. This elevated him into a shining constellation in the history of Chinese calligraphy. Secondly, he surpassed Fan Qin in several branches of learning. For example, his monograph *Wu Jing Shi Xue—On the Five Classics* was of a quality that Fan Qin was never able to achieve. But as a thorough scholar and artist, Feng Fang was too easily worked up, too simple-minded and tactless, too separated from reality and prone to follow his own fantasies and inclinations. At the beginning, he took the firm resolution to sell off one thousand *mu* (One Chinese *mu* equals to about 666. 7 square meters—the translator) of good farmland from his family holdings so as to be able to buy books and calligraphy models, and established a library of considerable scale before Fan Qin could set up his. But owing to his ignorance of the ways of the world, and the hypocrisy of his disciples, who often secretly tried to obtain his books by force or by trickery, and his lack of precautions against fire, an estimated sixty percent of his collection of books were stolen, and another large proportion lost in disastrous fires during his old age, so he ended up selling the remainder to Fan Qin, who did not have Feng Fang's literary and artistic talent, nor his defects in personality. The intuitive knowledge of culture possessed by both of them, when refined by Fan Qin's cool reasoning, embodied itself in sober social behavior. Obviously, Fan Qin had a stronger social personality, which enabled him to take good charge of the cultural cause. Pure artists or scholars were usually too stiff to do this kind of things well or at all.

Another book collector that can be compared with Fan Qin was his nephew Fan Dache. Influenced from childhood by his uncle, Fan Dache took after Fan Qin in many aspects. For example, he was a very competent official and served as an envoy abroad, while cherishing a passionate fondness for books. As a very learned man of good judgment on the value of books, he once collected many valuable books. His book collection was started mainly by two types of stimulation from his uncle: one was the infection of his uncle's book-loving example; another was his uncle's refusal or hesitation to grant Fan Dache's request to borrow a book. After this incident, he was determined to set up a library of his own to compete with that of his uncle. When the library was built several years later, he often invited Fan Qin to it and deliberately put some treasured private copies of rare books on the desk for Fan Qin to read freely. However, to all of his nephew's tricks, Fan Qin only gave an indifferent smile. Here the difference between the two book collectors, the uncle and the nephew, is clearly seen. Swayed mainly by petty personal feelings, the nephew's ultimate aim was very limited, though he could make the library a good enterprise. Once his library building was constructed and copies of rare editions not possessed by his uncle were collected, he felt comforted and satisfied. Unfortunately, the nephew's library lasted only a few generations and all of the books were lost over time; whereas the uncle's library, Tianyi Pavilion, stood intact with a peculiar strength. In fact, its longevity came from Fan Qin's iron will beyond personal feelings, hobbies, talent, emotion and time. This special will might appear too cold and severe for some all through the years, but it was just this that made Tianyi Pavilion last.

IV

The real trouble for book collectors usually came after their deaths.

Therefore the problem Fan Qin faced was how to turn his own will into an immovable family heritage. It might be said that the really moving and tragic history of Tianyi Pavilion began with Fan Qin's death. The history is so heartbreaking that it is hard to say whether the mission of protecting the library building is a kind of honor or toil lasting hundreds of years.

At the age of 80, when Fan Qin was at the end of his life, he sent for his eldest son and the dead second son's widow to arrange the inheritance affairs. Fan Qin, in his last breath, set a difficult problem for them. He put the inheritance into two shares, one consisting of ten thousand taels of silver and the other just the library, and let the two make their own choice.

This was indeed a strange way of dividing the inheritance properties. The ten thousand taels of silver would enable the proprietor to enjoy many good things; whereas a houseful of books could only be a heavy burden for its owner, for Fan Qin's life-long example already showed his descendants that none of the books in the collection could be sold. What is more, to keep the books in good condition would cost a lot of money. Why didn't Fan Qin divide the silver into two portions, each for one branch of the descendents? Why did he separate right from duty so definitely for the later generation to choose?

I believe that it must have taken dozens of years for the old man to decide on this special way of dividing the inheritance. As a matter of fact, this was a difficult problem he set for himself: either someone in his later generation would volunteer to be duty-bound and take up the painstaking task of maintaining the books without wanting anything else, or just let the books completely vanish with his own life. So he deliberately made his will unreasonable and left nothing profitable in terms of money to the branch of the descendants who was determined to inherit the books, for he knew clearly the smallest monetary touch would make the motivation to inherit the books impure. This kind of impurity could be expanded from generation to generation and they would ultimately follow the same disastrous fate of the other book collectors. On the other hand, he did not mean to insult or scorn the branch that would inherit the ten thousand taels of silver. He wanted an honest admission of the lack of confidence in such historical toil instead of a dishonest pledge. However, what he more wanted to hear just before his death were the words he looked forward to for years. He was not afraid of death, but at the moment he stared at their eyes in restless fear.

His eldest son Fan Dachong was the first to make clear his position and declared that he wished to inherit Tianyi Pavilion, where the collection of books was kept, and that he would lease some of his good farmland and use the rent to maintain both the books and the repository building.

In this way an endless relay began. Years later, Fan Dachong would make his will and then the son of Fan Dachong his own…with the will made by a later generation being more strict than the previous one. The more the family clan multiplied, the farther they were from the original motivation of collecting books. How to make every branch and every family of the large Fan clan generations later scrupulously abide by their ancestor Fan Qin's norm was really a difficult subject worth further investigation. At that time, every cultural cause spanning considerable years in history required continuation that was possible to be realized only by family inheritance. But the family multiplication was a constant procedure of splitting, alienation and independence. To make the later generations of later generations accept the hard instructions that required life-long dedication somehow violated the natural state of life. It was simply not rational to have the descendants carry on the impulse of an ancestor living hundreds of years earlier. Obviously, for many descendants of the Fan clan, Tianyi Pavilion almost became the object of worship. They protected, maintained and preserved it year after year with reverence and awe, but had no genuine understanding of the collection's purpose or value. According to today's mode of thinking, people might be lost in contemplation of their cultural consciousness which has been passed on from generation to generation while speaking highly of the Fan family's magnificent contributions. But I believe many indescribable psychological tragedies and family disputes must have taken place during the several hundreds of years. Much sympathy should be given to the family that lived below the special library for so many centuries.

Curiosity was sure to rise among the posterity of the Fan family about what it was like inside the building and what kinds of books were collected and whether some copies could be borrowed. Friends and relatives would pester them for entrance into the mysterious place worshipped for generations by the Fan family.

All these possibilities had long been predicted by Fan Qin and his successors. They had also anticipated the possible collapse on account of such entries and had taken measures to prevent it accordingly. They made strict penalty rules, forbidding the transgressor to take part in the sacrificial rites for ancestors, which at that time was the greatest disgrace, as good as a warning of family ostracism, much more severe than stick-flogging or whip-lashing. According to the penalty rules, the posterity who entered the building without any special reason should be forbidden to attend the family sacrificial rites three times. For those who took friends or relatives there and opened the bookcases, the prohibited time was a whole year; for those who lent books to outside branches or other families, three years; and for those who put the books in pawn, they would be forever denied the right to take part in family sacrificial rites in addition to a fine.

Here the event must be mentioned that has made me sad every time it comes to my mind. In the period of Jiaqing in the Qing Dynasty, there was a girl called Qian Xiuyun, who was the niece of Qiu Tieqing, the governor of Ningbo prefecture. The girl liked poems and books very much. In order to gain access to the collection of books preserved in Tianyi Pavilion, she let the governor act as a matchmaker and marry her into one branch of the Fan family. The modern sociologists might ask whether Miss Qian intended to marry a man or the books, but it seemed to me that in an era when marriages were mainly arranged according to the parents' interest and will, it was really moving for the girl to disregard money and power factors, and merely make use of the arrangement to read more books. Nevertheless, it had not occurred to her that she could be firmly denied the right to read the books even if she had become the daughter-in-law of the Fan family. One reason given was that the clan rule prohibited all women from entering the building; some others said it was because the Fan descendant she married actually belonged to a collateral branch of the family. Whatever was the real reason, the fact was that Qian Xiuyun never read any of the books in Tianyi Pavilion and finally died in melancholy.

Now, when I look up at the building, I cannot help but think of Qian Xiuyun's melancholic eyes. Indeed, a book-length of literary work can come out of this. Instead of picturing a normal marriage tragedy, it will describe how a girl struggled persistently and helplessly with her longing for cultural entertainment in an atmosphere marked by a total lack of humanism in China.

From the Fan family's standpoint, entries into the building and reading inside had to be strictly forbidden. Of course, it also frequently confused the Fan clan as to the use of such a library if all requests for entries and reading were refused.

According to the rules made by the family, entry into the building could only be allowed with unanimity no matter how many branches the family had multiplied into. The various keys to the front door of the building and to each bookcase were kept by different branches respectively, thus forming an interlocking management system. The absence of any of the branches would make it impossible to get access to the books. As any branch could exercise the veto, in the course of time they all started contemplating the ultimate value of Tianyi Pavilion.

Just at that time, the news came that the great scholar Huang Zongxi wanted to enter the building to read. This caused great agitation among all the branches of the family. Born in Yuyao, Huang Zongxi did not have the least blood relationship with the Fans and should firmly be denied entry as the rules indicated. Yet, in spite of the primitive media at that time, the Fans had long heard of the academic giant's respectable character, integrity, learning, and the great sensation caused by his peculiar and outstanding deeds in the government and among the public. His father, an important person on the Donglin party in the last years of the Ming Dynasty, was murdered by the eunuch clique headed by Wei Zhongxian. Later, when this clique was brought to trial, the nineteen-year-old Huang Zonxi indignantly beat up and stabbed the remnants of the overthrown clique with an awl. After that, he hunted and killed the murderer and issued a serious warning to Ruan Dacheng, an important member of the clique. All the things he did gave the people immense satisfaction. When the army of the Qing Dynasty marched down to the south, with two of his brothers he organized hundreds of young people still loyal to the dethroned Ming Dynasty to resist it. After the defeat of his desperate resistance, he devoted himself to academic study, writing books while giving lectures. By merging the national morality, justice and human dignity into academic learning to enlighten the people, he became a first-rate thinker and historian in the ancient Chinese academic field. In the process of pursuing his studies, he had visited and read in the Niu family's library The Building of Learning and in the Qi family's Indifferent House in Shaoxing. Now, he finally made up his mind to tap the front door of Tianyi Pavilion. Though he knew very well about the Fan family's most strict rules, he came and tried in 1673, the twelfth year of Emperor Kangxi.

Quite unexpectedly, it was unanimously agreed by all branches of the family that Mr. Huang Zongxi could enter the library and read closely all the books in it. To me, this event stands as a verification of the cultural character and morals of the Fan family. As book collectors, they were not rated high in academic and political circles, yet they offered their much-treasured keys to this particular person. The noble personality of the huge Fan clan was vividly embodied in this choice and decision. With one after another copper lock opened, Huang Zongxi, in his long robe and cloth shoes, quietly climbed the staircase in the building. 1673 thus became the most shining year in the history of Tianyi Pavilion.

At the library, Huang Zongxi actually leafed through all of the books. He then made a title catalogue for the books that could seldom be found and wrote an article named "Tianyi Pavilion and Its Collection of Books." This further connected Tianyi Pavilion with this famous scholar.

From then on, the Fan family made a rule of opening the library to really important scholars. But the execution of the rule was still very strict.

Only about a dozen scholars, whose names were important enough to appear in the cultural history of China, ever had their permission to enter the library during 200 years.

Owing to this practice, Tianyi Pavilion did show its significance though the chance to show it was so small. In fact, there was always a sharp contradiction between the feudal family's blood relationship of inheritance and the social needs of academic circles. There was also the uncompromising predicament the book-collector had to face: he should either leave the books untouched in order to preserve them as long as he could or bring their social value into play to wear them away or lose them. It seemed that the most stringent choice made by the Fan family to open the library was only a makeshift in this dilemmatic and helpless situation. However, this nation-wide strict choice was already much beyond any ordinary family clan's horizon and function.

It was not until Emperor Qianlong decided to compile *Si Ku Quan Shu*, a huge set of encyclopedias based on the four ancient classifications, that a new direction was found for the solution of the contradictions. Qianlong instructed every province to look for old or missing books and let all book collectors, especially those living in the south of the Yangtse River, contribute their books. Accordingly, the Fan family dedicated more than 600 categories of valuable ancient books, of which 96 were included in this body of the imperial collection, and 370 were listed in the index of books. To express his gratitude to the Fan family for their contribution, Qianlong praised and bestowed rewards on them many times and ordered the libraries under construction all over the country to imitate the structure of Tianyi Pavilion.

Tianyi Pavilion therefore became very famous. Although most of the books the Fans presented were not sent back, the books found their places in the national encyclopedia and the libraries made by imperial order. Hence it seems to me a distortion that some writings and articles regarded the Fans' contribution of books under Qianlong's instruction as a great catastrophe for Tianyi Pavilion. The ultimate aim of collecting books was not "to preserve" but to make them spread widely. Even the imperial book-compiling project had to draw on a lot of books from Tianyi Pavilion, and this served as an undisputed evidence of the success of Fan Qin and the library: a family collection turned into a nationally regarded treasure.

V

In due course, Tianyi Pavilion entered modern times. It may seem strange to say, but everything in China seemed to become very queer in this historical period. The ancient building then began its new adventure.

First, when the army of the Taiping Heavenly Kingdom attacked Ningbo in the 19th century, the local thieves tore open the building wall and stole some books, which were later sold to a paper workshop. It was said that someone once paid high prices and bought some books back from the workshop, but the books he rescued from the workshop were later burned up by an unexpected fire.

This calamity proved to be a bad omen for Tianyi Pavilion's later misfortune. The problem the Fan family now faced was no longer whether or not to let a famous scholar enter the library but how to guard against burglars and thieves, their chief adversaries at that time.

In 1914, a thief called Xue Jiwei somehow sneaked into the building, resting quietly by day and stealing books by night while eating only dates he had brought with him. A boat stopped on the river just outside of the east wall, transferring all the stolen books. This theft robbed Tianyi Pavilion of almost half its valuable books, which gradually appeared in some of the bookstores in Shanghai.

Xue Jiwei's stealing was quite different from those that took place during the peasant uprising of Taiping Heavenly Kingdom. Not only was the number of books stolen huge and the stealing process better arranged, but also the thieves had some contact with the bookstores in Shanghai and they obviously acted on the booksellers' instigation. I think it stands for a sort of evil symbol that booksellers in the modern metropolis would resort to this way of misappropriating an ancient library. Fan Qin, who had once cudgeled his brains to take every measure to protect the library, had never thought that theft could be the main peril of the library since they had such solid walls at that time and therefore did not give sufficient consideration to methods of theft-prevention. It was really impossible for Fan Qin to imagine the arrival of such modern times and the means the merchants would use during their primitive accumulation period for capitals. So bit by bit the bookcases were emptied. On the floor upstairs where Ms. Qian Xiuyun could only look up from some distance but never be able to climb, and where Mr. Huang Zongxi so cautiously treaded, there was merely a pile of pits of dates left behind by the thief.

When Mr. Zhang Yuanji, who then took charge of the Commercial Press, heard of the Tianyi Pavilion calamity and found out that some booksellers had made arrangements to sell the books stolen from Tianyi Pavilion to foreigners, he immediately offered huge funds to buy them back and kept them in the Fragrant Building of the Oriental Library, which began to become famous in the cultural circle for taking in the precious books from Tianyi pavilion. Many important scholars absorbed in spiritual nourishment there. But, as known by many people, this library was ruined under the bombs of the Japanese aggressor troops.

This was, of course, even further beyond the expectations of Fan Qin, living centuries earlier. His special incantation against fire as implied by the Chinese characters "Tianyi" at last had lost its enchantment.

VI

But undoubtedly, the intuitive knowledge and good intention shown by Fan Qin and his descendants have not entirely fallen into oblivion in the contemporary age. Apart from Mr. Zhang Yuanji, many other warm-hearted people tried to protect this dilapidated building and prevent its ruin. Nowadays this has incontrovertibly become a social project, since one family or one clan's efforts are inadequate. Fortunately, Tianyi Pavilion was re-enriched and renovated on a grand scale in the 1930's, 1950's, 1960's, and 1980's. It has become a major repository of cultural relics and a tourist resort of Ningbo. The ancient books kept in Tianyi Pavilion now require systematizing and collating; yet in this age marked by concentrated information and convenience of cultural interchange, their real significance no longer lies in their contents, which can provide the society with knowledge, but in the kind of symbol of classic cultural cause they always stand for. This reminds people of the painstaking process of preserving and handing down the Chinese culture, and sets them to thinking of an ancient nation's cultural longing embodied in sorrow and sacredness.

We, in essence of life, unquestionably belong to the creators of modern culture, but at the same time are doubtlessly inheritors of the traditional culture. Therefore we are more or less the descendents of Tianyi Pavilion's ancient system, though we don't belong to the Fan family.

When I came up the stairs of Tianyi Pavilion, I was very slow in taking every step. I asked myself over and over again: "Have you really come? What generation of the Chinese scholars do you belong to?"

Seldom had I had such a serious yet peaceful mind when I had visited other places. In this building, a very old scholar specializing in edition studies nervously presented to me two books of Ming Dynasty block-printed edition, one being Records of Test Winners and another being the ancient annals of Shanghai. After leafing them through, a great feeling of awe surged up within me: without these only existing copies, many aspects of China's history would be difficult, if not impossible to find out. My thoughts then wandered to another question: whether or not the history of Tianyi Pavilion needs further exploration. Mr. Pei Minghai passed me a booklet entitled *Historical Stories of Ningbo* written by Xu Jizi, Zheng Xuepu and Yuan Yuanlong. One article in the booklet introduced with a clear and matter-of-fact narrative all the vicissitudes of Tianyi Pavilion and enabled me to gain knowledge of the historical facts that had long been unknown to me. Yet, it seems to me that it is worth writing a great and long epic for Tianyi Pavilion. When will our men of letters turn their attention to this old building and its courtyard? When should the spirit and the hundreds of years of history of the Fan clan and many other clans be revealed to the modern world?

The translator's notes:

About the author: Yu Qiuyu (1946 –) is a well-known professor and experimentalist in essay writing, who has published quite a number of collections of essays, which have caused great sensations in China in recent years.

About the essay: This essay was published in *Harvest*, Issue 3, 1991. By talking about the construction, maintenance and vicissitudes of the well-known ancient private library in Ningbo, Zhejiang Province, the author tries to reexamine the historical fate of the Chinese culture and the unique personality of the traditional Chinese scholars.

The River I Always Remember

Zhou Peihong

Till now, whenever I close my eyes, I can still see clearly that beautiful river flowing quietly among the green mountains of Shangyu, Zhejiang Province. In east Zhejiang, a place in Southern China, it's not rare to see such a river, why should I have just remembered that Cao Er River?

Is it because the river is exceptionally clear and quiet? Or because the river's name was taken after that of a young girl? Or because it has a sad story hidden in it?

I can never tell. In one's memory there are always unaccountable reasons that tenaciously retain some accidental occasions. Perhaps, the answer to the riddle just lies in the clear water of the Cao-er River, only I cannot see it when glancing at it.

My last trip to Shangyu was not to purposely visit Cao Er River. But, When I came out the railway station, caught a glimpse of it from some distance in this town paved by gray slab-stones, I was greatly attracted by it. At first, it looked like a long narrow strip of white silk, and then appeared like an unfolded roll of silver satin. When the river flowing passed me, the water seemed suddenly to make the sky far and high, and the mountains on both banks of it low and sliding. The water was not noisy, and foams of breaking waves could hardly be seen. There was just an unparalleled pure world that was constantly and slowly unfolding. The unaccountable thin waves on the surface of the river were shining like thousands scales of fish, which seemed to be cutting the azure of the mountains to present a deformed picture. White clouds seemed to have stopped drifting, waiting to be cleansed by the light reflected from the water. Everything appeared fresh, cool, transparent, and unsullied. I suddenly realized what the Chinese phrase "green hills and clear waters—picturesque scenery" really referred to.

The gray slab-stone road of the town was close to the river. Ascending a little higher, one can see the green moss and water plants on the shallower parts of it. On the surface of the river it was empty, only the quiet constant flow of the water showed the eternity. A few boats were lying bottom up on the beach, basking in the sun. Not one single boat broke the quiet of the water. Cao Er River was just as good as a gigantic piece of jasper, with no crack at all.

I could not help holding my breath, for fearing to blow away the almost condensed beauty. I just stepped lightly on the road which went the same direction with the river.

However, this is not the Cao Er River I have imagined. It should not be so beautiful, gentle and soft. In the color picture-story books I read as a child, it was a wild river with boundless turbulent, roaring waves, often cutting branches of trees and even rendering the sky gloomy and frightful. The ancient fourteen-year-old girl Cao Er just appeared in such a scene. She seemed to be in a boat, or walk along the river, stretching out her arms towards the water, calling her father who had fallen into the water and could never come back, and searching for his corpse. She was not able to find it. Seven days and nights later, she herself was drowned in the river. According to the book, she chose to plunge into the water to get drowned. She was therefore named "the filial daughter" and became well known. At that time, I could not understand what is "filialness", but just keep that river in mind, a river that cruelly and fearfully engulfed the life of a lonely young girl.

That river is now just before me, but the imagination and the reality cannot be identical. What is the true state of the Cao Er River? Maybe it has both states, but the history has grown old and the river can always be renewed.

I walked on and trod on the big gray hard and cold stone block of Temple of Cao Er, the Filial Daughter. When striding over it, I felt the huge character "filialness" on the horizontal board pressed on me like a great intangible weight. Though the temple hall was spacious, yet the up-turned eaves, the carved beams, the dark thick pillars and the black roof made of dark tiles often blocked the sight, and gloom gave out from the innermost part, with the smell of rotten wood and very old house. In spite of all this unpleasant impression, I walked into the hall.

After I restored my sight that failed for the sudden darkness, I saw myself standing in the middle of a broad veranda of stone tablets. Many years ago, Cao Er was buried here. It was to commemorate her that this temple was built. All through the following dynasties, high praises of her by celebrities were carved on numerous tablets, which, like unaccountable memorial archways, lifted this young girl who died early to some unbelievable height. Such raised, the colored statue of Cao Er appeared in bigger size on the altar of the main hall, which reminded people of the frequently seen Guan Yu, the heroic God of Wealth and Guanyin, the Goddess of

Mercy in rural areas. Her eyes, similar to all the other statues, were dull and blank, and did not really look at anything. Her shoulders drooped limply, even the colorful dress and the two black buns of hair (all made of mud) could not bring any vividness to her. The altar table showed that she had been worshiped all the years by many people. Till the present time, on March 3 of each lunar year, people would still swarm into the temple to worship her. Persons from far away places would lie everywhere in the temple to spend the night. Many even made use of the gray slab-stone road for the night's sleep. I cannot help thinking if it is really Cao Er—the desperate, helpless young girl who loved her father so deeply that they worship? She once wept so bitterly for her only parent, but where one can find her tears, cries, fears and lament now?

The statue of Cao Er is right in the middle of the altar, standing on each side of it are smaller statues of young girls, one of whom is called "Zhu Er" and another also has the word "Er" in her name. In Shangyu area, a lot of girls' given name is "Er" (In China, family name is before the given name—the translator). After Cao Er became well known, this fad of using "Er" as the given name of a girl is more popular. It is said that the two "Er"s mentioned above just followed Cao Er's example to die as a filial daughter at a very early age. Therefore, they, too, got their places in this temple for the filial daughter and were worshiped together with Cao Er by later generations. Their life stories are carved before the altar as well. An antithetical couplet is engraved in full-length on the pillars, only I could not bear to read it closely. Beautiful flowers of young lives were withered and fell so early, for which I could only lament silently in the mind. How can an abstract word "filialness" summarize the vivid and rich existence of life and the unfortunate and tragic death?

I felt kind of heavy-laden—Cao Er and girls like her were not only drowned by the river water, but by the veranda of tablets and the inscriptions.

Stepping out of the temple, I saw again the Cao Er River, which was spangling with golden stars under the shining sun, flowing forward in dazzling golden color.

The river opened its bosom wider and wider to me, and the thin ripples became clearer. I let my insteps covered by the moist and warm sand and then walked into the water barefooted. Under the lukewarm surface, the water was cool and ran rapidly like some impulsive force. This kind of water was really unusual. When as beautiful and tender as a young lady, it would splash, wet Cao Er's clothes, making her cry with surprise and laugh a lot. When wind and rain pushed the river water forward with force among the mountains, it could also produce huge waves. At such a time, it would wet Cao Er's hair, pull her clothes, swept all her hopes, and then swallow up the exhausted girl. After all, the river water once heard the laughs and weeps of young Cao Er, witnessed different expressions of hers. The stories recorded by the river water must be richer than those engraved on the stone tablets. The tablet for Cao Er, might be better made of the water than stone.

Several local girls walked down along the gray slab-stone road of the town. They, having pink cheeks, looked fifteen or sixteen years old. Each of them rolled up their trousers. Seeing me wade in the water, they smiled and shouted: "The water is icy, take care of your health." Meanwhile, they themselves splashed the water with feet in laughter. Their voices are as fresh and simple as the green grass on the bank. Do they also have "Er" as the given name?

Turbulent waves, which were caused by fresh flows in the depths of water, appeared and Cao Er River immediately became more vivid. I could not understand its language, but I could feel that it seemed to stimulate my imaginations, making me to go beyond what was tangible and fixed, to seek for another kind of truth, soft, formless, changeable and perpetual like the river water.

The translator's notes:

About the author: Zhou Peihong (1951 –) is a senior editor, essayist and writer. She has published quite a number of books and is often regarded as one of the representatives of the new essays.

About the essay: This essay was written in May, 1989. Later it was included in her collection of essays called *Imprints in My Mind* published in 1991. The translation was based on the edition of 100 *Essays during the 60 Years in China* published in 2009. In the essay the author reexamines and criticizes the traditional values of regarding young girls' unnecessary self-sacrifice as being filial.

Woman Matchmakers in China

Tu Ao

In earlier years China was rich in woman matchmakers. Their stereotypical images often appeared in movies, dramas, stories and novels:

Their faces are painted as white as gourds covered with thick frost,

Their dresses are as colorful as costumes for actresses,

With one or two kicks of their feet, they get on the *kang* (a kind of brick or earthen bed that can be heated by faggots in the winter—the translator) gracefully,

When they pull their sleeve cuffs, they mean they are waiting for the pay...

Curling their lips, they were capable of saying the sharpest words as well as the sweetest ones. They were reputed to be ridiculous and disgusting, and girls always tried to avoid them as if they were pestilences; whereas their parents took them as respectable guests.

However, these are not the true pictures of woman matchmakers, who actually had their own happiness and sadness. Degraded as they were, they tried to accomplish a sacred task all the same. The woman matchmakers were really such a group, in the mountains, plains, and all over China.

The matchmakers were usually middle-aged or old women; few young girls acted the part. Women, when reaching the middle age or growing old, would become very outspoken in character. They would wear their wisdom on their faces and all their wrinkles would indicate their courage and qualification. They engaged themselves to do the matching either of their own will, or under someone's entrustment.

The typical matchmaker's first practice in matching always seemed like her first experience of meeting her own would-be husband, inevitably marked with dodging and stuttering. She could never tell clearly what she meant, nor could she give up the attempt. Thinking of the great trust and warm reception given to her by the client, the woman matchmaker would close her eyes and ask for a glass of wine, swallow it in one gulp like a man, then with a face as red as a boiled crab she would begin the business: "Great aunt, please allow me to venture a question. Is your daughter engaged or not? If yes, you can take my question as sheer nonsense; if not, what about the sixth son of the Li family?" In fact, the girl's parents were much younger than the woman matchmaker, yet as the old saying goes, even soldiers won't hit the man with all smiles; the form of address only aimed to please the addressee.

Still these words could often meet with sharp irony accompanied by tapping the *kang* with the handle of a small broom: "Old sister, you'd better have your little feet rested! My family is a small temple that cannot afford the lotus throne that brings such an honored go-between like you!" On hearing this, the woman would flee out of the front door as quickly as she could. She would not dare to turn round a bit until she covered one kilometer. The worst thing would be leaving on the *kang* the parcel that contained her client's gifts to the girl's family. Knowing that the unsuccessful first contact plus the loss of the gifts would give her a very bad reputation, the woman could do nothing but force herself to go back, with a cold breath and a long face. As she reached the front door of which she had just come out and was ready to tap it again, the door opened automatically with a creak and the parcel was thrown out with the words: "Take it away! We don't want it to dirty our *kang*!" The words were fierce enough to make the matchmaker stagger. Tottering, she fled again.

When she came back home, her own children would criticize: "You are asking for trouble yourself!"

This was a worse blow, and with a very confused mind, she flung herself into the *kang* full of the smell of sweat and would not want to eat anything for three days.

There were also some exceptions when they met with families that treated them politely, telling them the truth in kind words or accepting their proposals immediately. On these occasions the woman matchmaker's face would light up like that of a happy little girl, and she would trot hurriedly to her client's house, where all the family members, realizing the match had been made, began to prepare the tea and meal in a bustle for the woman who had just rendered them the great service. The woman, when led in like a moon among a group of stars, would sit with her legs crossing most gracefully, drink and eat assuredly and proudly, while giving all kinds of orders as if she were now Empress Dowager Cixi, who had administered affairs of the state behind a screen.

This was the glorious victory of the woman matchmaker.

However, the woman matchmaker's road to success was very exceptional. After the very first matchmaking, whether it was glorious or obscure, they would treasure it just as a craftsman who was holding a drill with diamond tip, even if he had no jade to work on, he would never give the drill to others; or like a bride to be sent on a sedan to the bridegroom, who, though crying or weeping, would just let herself be carried away. The only difference was that the victorious matchmakers would make more successes; whereas the obscure ones would again get nowhere.

Although it is difficult to tell whether the matchmakers can be regarded as architects, they did build bridges between unmarried men and girls.

In the old times, those who acted as matchmakers were usually poor women. Although they ordinarily wore colorless rags, they would manage to dress up for the matchmaking business.

Appearance was always important for this business. The matchmaker would somehow represent her client's status and therefore must be well-dressed. The matchmaker's make-up and good clothes were partly for her reputation and partly for that of others.

The attractive clothes were necessary for her because she was welcomed as an important person, who was supposed to speak of elegant things, which certainly required decent clothes and graceful manners.

A well-dressed matchmaker was also to the client's advantage because the client's financial status could well be reflected through the matchmaker's appearance. It is said that once a quick-witted woman wore her usual kitchen clothes to act as the matchmaker. When she entered the prospective bride's boudoir, she was puzzled by the old couple's behavior— instead of giving her a warm reception, they just covered their noses and whispered to each other. Just at this time, the crisp voice of a girl came from behind the screen: "What a shabby matchmaker! The man must live in sheer poverty. What a shame!" On hearing this, the woman could say nothing but left the room quietly, feeling very hurt.

Consequently, the poor and homely women who made a living by act-
ing as matchmakers had to make use of all resources at home to buy good
clothes, just as actresses must have proper costumes when they put on performances. In order to have enough money for the clothes, the woman used
up her many year's personal savings or borrowed men's hard-earned money.
It was from just this that the ill name stemmed. People usually said that the
matchmakers depended on their clients for good meals and for good
clothes, and that, glib-tongued, they did their best to draw out every coin
of their clients' and were really a group of lazy and evil women, who were
always very particular about what they ate and wore. In fact, shrewish as
they could be, they were very sensitive about their reputation. Their profession often required them to stand for many unbearable things and make
lamentable sacrifices.

After obtaining the good clothes, the matchmaker had to make up her
face in order that it would go with the clothes. However, few of them knew
the principles of aesthetics, and they just made a sight of themselves. A
bored poet wrote the lines:

Shamelessly the old women put flowers on their heads;

Sight of this even makes young people blush!

Among mockery, jeering and laughter, the matchmaker went to and
fro, in sunset or against the old tree, busy making matches for others. Isn't
it both pitiable and admirable!

Matchmaking was in essence a drama-like art: it had its own patterns
and procedures. In it the matchmaker acted both as the actress and the director.

The matchmakers had many means to accomplish their tasks. The following are the methods most commonly heard and seen.

First, it was matchmaking through talking. This was often meant for reasonable families that cared a lot about their reputation. The matchmaker, when coming into such families, would brush the dust off her clothes, take the cup of tea respectfully and then talk like reeling off raw silk from cocoons while sipping her tea. When the tea had made her feel hot or the talk made her very pleased, she knew her chance had come and then decided the young man's and the young girl's fate in a few words. Once the match was made, everyone would be happy; if the match could not be agreed on, they usually ended up peacefully, and the matchmaker was seen off politely and gently.

Second, there was matchmaking through smiling, which was often applied to powerful and wealthy families. The matchmaker was always timid and nervous when going to those families. Smiling from the beginning to the end and being very cautious about everything, she would first present a lot of compliments to the host and hostess to coax them to drop their pretentious airs a little and look more pleased, and then she seized the opportune moment to raise the proposal. If the matchmaker was fortunate, the host and hostess would give her considerable quantities of gifts, ostensibly out of their gratitude, but actually to display their richness. If the matching proposal was not considered proper by the host family, the matchmaker had to say endless nice words and then flee out of the house while taking special precautions against the fierce dog by the doorway.

The third was matchmaking through quarreling. This was the situation often encountered in a girl's family with lots of women—sisters-in-law, aunts and grandmas. When entering such a family, the matchmaker was just like a scholar who met a group of soldiers who could make a lot of trouble. Not only did they try to draw out every bit of information about the proposer, but they were also very skilled in bargaining over the betrothal gifts as if their girl was a fairy maiden about to be worthlessly engaged. Surrounded by all the women in the family like a piece of sore meat under the pecks of a flock of crows, the matchmaker only wished she could return to her mother's womb. It was a fight with her back to the river—a fight to win or die for the matchmaker, who had to defend her own dignity and the proposer's interest through every means, quarreling or fighting, just like a warrior in a battlefield.

The fourth was matchmaking through cursing. The matchmaker, when confronted with some rude and impolite family, would turn into a shrew and combat poison with poison, deliberately belittling the girl's family for their unfitness to marry their daughter to a good man. She would say that her arrival was actually an act of condescension, and if she was offended, she would make the girl and her family notorious. As matchmakers were usually united, the girl's family had to make concessions for fear that the threats may really come to fruition.

The last common matchmaking method was composed of sitting and weeping. This often happened when a second marriage was proposed to a widow. If a man fell in love with a young widow, some dramatic scene of matchmaking would follow. As soon as the widow made out what the woman had come for, she would immediately burst into a stormy curse. Totally dumbstruck, the go-between could do nothing but sit straight and listen attentively. Right after the storm, the widow would let loose a flood of tears, telling the visitor her hardship, loneliness and helplessness, which usually made the matchmaker join her weeping. When they cried to their hearts' content, the matchmaker would take up the subject through persuading. Even if the proposal was not agreed on, the go-between showed no sign of leaving and kept sitting and talking. Too often it was the widow who finally gave in and let the matchmaker fulfill her task.

In fact few of the above-mentioned matchmaking methods were used alone. It was normally through resorting to several means by turns that the matchmaker's aim could be attained.

Also like enacting dramas, matchmaking was a very expressive art and had its own script. This occupation was in fact a combination of hardship and humiliation; no praise was ever give to it. The matchmaker could only sometimes quietly enjoy a bit of happiness alone.

Normally people took matchmaking as a sort of profession; while some were quite addicted to it.

To help someone to fulfill his wish was a good thing and deserved some rewards. Hence in the matchmaking profession, there were some unwritten rules: when a match was made, rewards would be accepted; whereas if a proposal was not agreed on, the matchmaker should return the gifts she had received earlier. The Chinese people always believed that rewards and punishments must have reasons. As matchmakers were ordinary people, how could they be exceptions?

Matchmaking belonged to the long-existing Chinese feudal cultural tradition. Nowadays, though the reform is in full swing, still we cannot expect it to stop the inertia of the traditional custom like the brakes of a bike. In the mountain areas, matches are still made by go-betweens. Some young people may have already found their loves or lovers, yet on the betrothal ceremony, a go-between should be invited to formally make the match. The procedure represents custom; it's not too gratifying, nor detestable, but adds poetic flavor to a solitary village. This alone is the matchmaker's function today. However, it cannot be denied that matchmakers have performed some meritorious service to the continuation of the Chinese nation and the prosperity of the Chinese people all through the history. This special group has really been the Venus in China!

If a woman were too addicted to matchmaking, she would become a nuisance.

Addiction often resulted in haste. If no clients came to her, she might go around to look for the unmarried young men for business arrangements. The young man she found probably already had a girl after his heart and appeared rather indifferent to this kind of thing. When persuaded eagerly and offered many suggestions, he might casually consent to have a match made for him through the go-between. These words immediately set the matchmaker to busy mediation. Finally, when a suitable girl was found and recommended to the young man, he only shook his head and if pressed, he would accuse the woman of being meddlesome, leaving her very puzzled. This failed match was really a humiliation for the marriage broker.

Sometimes, when the addicted go-between saw a gauntly girl walking about under the shade of a willow, she always took her to be worrying about marriage and saw a prospective client. She would volunteer to her parents to be the matrimonial agent for the girl. Yet quite unexpectedly, instead of giving her their consent, the parents might take affront at the offer and simply burst out: "Do you think our daughter has no arm or leg?" meaning that although their daughter was not a princess, she had no marriage problem at all. The matchmaker had again humiliated herself...

Whenever an unhappy marriage occurred, a husband or wife would inevitably bear resentment against the matchmaker. In Hebei province there went a folk song called the "Hatred for the Matchmaker," in which a description of the happy old days and hard present life was followed by the curse:

The matchmaker is wicked and deceitful,

May the red cloth she received become ash,

May her legs be rotten or broken,

May she never arrange marriages again!

It was easy to, rather than blame the feudal culture, attribute all the wrongs to the matchmakers, who were in fact also the victims of the feudal culture and happened to act as a carrier of the culture. It was not fair for them!

On the other hand, the matchmakers are lovably kind in the Chinese classic love novels *The Story of the West Wing-room* and *Flowers as the Go-between.*

Facts showed that the matchmakers were a group of unyielding persons. When setbacks were met, instead of losing their fighting will and courage, they threw away all disguise and even refused to receive gifts, which made them more carefree, bold and assured in persuading or arguing. If proposals were agreed on, well and good; if not, the matchmakers owed nothing to others. Since China's liberation in 1949, a radical change has taken place in the matchmakers' psychological state; matchmaking has become a duty or obligation.

Recently, the modern "machine matchmakers" and "collective matchmakers" have come into being. The matchmaking standards and methods are so many as to be dazzling:

The structure of knowledge;

The types of disposition;

The stored love signals and procedures;

The microcomputers...

Now, the number of matchmakers is much expanded and their service modernized!

Still, it's always the time to say good-bye to the matchmaker when a wedding ceremony is held.

Just because the matchmaker is easy to be forgotten, I, a writer behind the times, have written all this about the matchmakers.

I'm ready to receive all the curses from the matchmakers and the common people!

The translator's notes:

About the author: Tu Ao (1963 –) is the pen-name of Shi Changyi, a notable writer living in the suburb of Beijing. He has published several collections of essays.

About the translation and the essay: The translation above is based on the edition that was published in *Essays*, Issue 2, 1987. In the essay the author provided more aspects of the traditional women matchmakers than people usually read, heard or saw them in books, movies, and dramas.

Part Ⅲ

The Small-fruited Fig Trees of My Birthplace

Huang Helang

On the slope to the left of my house, stand two old small-fruited fig trees (this kind of tree can also be translated as banyan—the translator), which cover the ground with a great deal of shade. Their green leaves provide a pleasant sight among the lead gray cement buildings. When in scorching summer, they would give an enchanting sense of coolness. From some time which I cannot exactly recall, a small level ground has been laid out under the trees, children's slide and pavilion built, Chinese fan palm and flowers planted in a surrounding way, all serve to make a tiny playing ground for children. Perhaps it is owing to my special intimacy with the small-fruited fig trees that I often bring my little son here for a walk in the morning or the evening, or just sit on the green bench, watching the children play while feeling carefree and content.

One day, I was so pleased that I acted like a child, and plucked a green leaf from the branch of the tree, with which I made a small whistle. I tried to blow it, it sounded monotonous and simple. My little son jumped excitedly and got it and then blew it with all his might. Attracted by the sound, a little black unknown dog drew near, with its little tail swaying comfortably and its eyes fixing on the little player. My son stopped blowing, the dog ran away with disappointment; he blew again, the dog drew near once more⋯This made my son chuckle a lot, flush appearing on his usual pink and white face.

My mind suddenly became a little bird, flying away from the sound of the whistle, over the blurring water and the vast mountains, and then lighted on one of the familiar small-fruited fig trees of my birthplace. I seemed to see again the thick and tall trunks, the moving tassels and the dense clouds of green leaves. In spring, the tender leaves used to be as transparent as jasper, shaking like eardrops and the sparkling dews would fall in the golden morning sunshine.

I cherish the memory of the clear brook that runs from the surrounding mountain of my birthplace and passes the small-fruited fig trees, the color cobblestones at the bottom of the brook, the quacking ducks on the surface of it, the young girls washing clothes in it and getting water from it; I also cherish the memory of the white stone bridge under the small-fruited fig trees, the engraved stone tablets at the ends of the bridge, and the little stone lions on the bridge railings, which are quite glossy because of people's frequent touches. The gurgling water of the brook brought away the years of my childhood, all my memory seem to have carved in the bridge, and stories I still remember are as many as the leaves of the small-fruited fig trees⋯

The two small-fruited fig trees standing at the end of bridge were very different: one was straight with exuberant leaves; another grew in the unusual "s" shape, its branches full of joints stretched out over the brook——we therefore gave it the name "the hunchback". What's more special about the latter is that the curved part of the trunk was hollow from burning and looked like a horizontal trough of over 3 meters. Yet, this tree was still alive, its dense twigs and leaves became upright and pointed to the sky over the other bank of the brook. In early years, we children all cherished special affection towards "the hunchback", and we used to regard the trough in its trunk as a "boat". Some of us would climb and enter it and then take bamboo poles for the oars to row. We used to row in this way with all our might though we knew that the "boat" would not move an inch. According to our childish dream, this "boat" would bring us to the vast green fields, round the hillside with burning azalea, pass through the orange grove with sweet-smelling little white flowers, head for the wide rivers, vast oceans, and faraway beautiful places…

Sometimes we would ask: how could the hunchback be burned to such a condition? According to old persons, once upon a time a large snake was hiding in this cave of the tree. Later it became a dragon and wanted to fly up to the heaven. However, because it wounded man and livestock and thus violated the laws of the heaven, the Jade Emperor who governs the heaven decided to punish it. So one night, the black clouds were pressing low and the fierce wind was blowing and trees shook wildly. A mighty lightening cut open the tree trunk like a sharp sword, and peals of thunder were rumbling threateningly. This small-fruited fig tree suddenly caught fire. The raging flames burned the snake alive. When the following downpour finally stopped the fire, there left this hollow trough in part of the trunk… This is a story told by the oldest man in the village whose beard was much like the tassels of the small-fruited fig tree. As we believed he was as old as the small-fruited fig trees, we believed his story as well.

On days we didn't quite know, we saw some women come to the trees to burn joss sticks and paper made to resemble money as an offering. What wishes did they pray this tree god for? I can only remember that when a child had face tinea, the mother would bring him to the tree, cut the trunk and applied the milky liquid that oozed out of it to the tinea. Some days later, the tinea seemed to have disappeared. The most unforgettable thing is that when the Spring Festival came, my grandma would ask me to climb up "the hunchback" to snap a few twigs of this ever-green tree, which she would plant into the cooked rice in the pot in order to offer as an sacrifice to ancestors. On such occasions, my kindly grandma would walk shakily to the stone bridge on her bounded small feet——"the three-inch lily." While watching me climb up the tree, she would tell me again and again to be careful. Although trembling with fear, I would pretend to be carefree and often wave to her the twigs I broke off from the tree proudly.

The long slabs of stone paved around the small-fruited fig trees are a-mong the things always to be recalled. In summer, they used to be the most desired "thrones" and "cool beds". At noon, when the subtropical sun made the interior of the houses as hot as having flames and the exterior ground so scorched, only this spot covered by the two small-fruited fig trees that were like huge umbrellas could resist the unbearable heat, provide a little coolness which would more or less relieve the by-passers walking on the hot stone board from the heat. In the evening, when the people fin-ished the whole day's work, they would lie down on the long slabs of stone washed clean by water from the brook, talking freely about the ancient no-vels, such as *The Three Kingdoms*, *Water Margin*, while enjoying the eve-ning breeze. They also talked about exceptional things that happened near-by or in remote places, about the growth of the crops and harvests to be ex-pected··· Whenever in the right mood, someone would play the two-stringed bowed musical instrument and sang in bold and unconstrained sound some songs smack of wildness, thus enjoying a little comfort and content in the years full of hardships.

What magic did the old small-fruited fig trees have to gather so many villagers around them? It was not moving language, not luring smile, but only the silent branches that stretched out like huge wings and served as shelter for people in the wind and rain, gave them shade in summer, thus protecting those simple and hard-working villagers.

I especially cherish the memory of the pleasant summer nights under the trees. Someone would wrap himself with thin sheets and sleep right on the slab of the stone, others would bring a few wood pieces to put one end on a bench and the other end right on the railing of the bridge to make a bed, which was then covered by a straw mat. I liked so much to sleep there with the adults, look at the dark shadow of the trees above, and talk in the mind with the smiling stars in the sky in such mysterious and tranquil atmosphere. On the moonlit nights, mountains and fields usually appeared to be enveloped in transparent fine gauze, everything looked as unreal as a dream or fairyland. Occasionally when I was half asleep, it seemed that the goddess of the moon flew over on a piece of cloud with the fragrance of the osmanthus, which would be spread through the branches of the small-fruited fig trees. The water under the bridge would sound like singing a sweet lullaby, which, together with the soft touch of the night breeze, would always make people get into sleep… Sometimes when awake in the morning, one would feel a touch of coolness, find the hair wetted by the dew, and the pillow missing. It usually turned out that the pillow had dropped into the river and then got aground among the cobbles, saturated and swollen with water…

These days will never come back again. It seems that I have just woken from a dream, though still with coolness from the shade of the small-fruited fig trees. I see that this is a long sleep that has lasted 30 years, and I am already thousands kilometers away from my birthplace! The small-fruited fig trees at the end of the bridge have also been weather-beaten. It is said that "the hunchback" finally fell into the flood water of the brook after a violent typhoon, thus finishing its course of life. It is fortunate the other small-fruited fig tree still remains and continues to provide protecting shade to the villagers in need. My childhood pals who entered the hollow part of the tree and took it for the boat and rowed with all their strength have all grown up. It is most likely that they still cherish the memory of the small-fruited fig trees like me no matter what far-away places their boats of life have brought them to. It is also most likely that they will again sit on the stone board surrounding the tree and tell the unending legend of it as their ancestors. However, the old man whose beard was much like the tassels of the small-fruited fig tree and who used to tell stories under the trees has already passed away. My grandma who used to ask me to get twigs from the trees has also passed away for a long time. Only the stone lions on the railings of the bridge, still listen to the sound of the flow of the brook.

"Dad, Dad, make more whistles for me!" I noticed that my little son also plucked some leaves from the tree and now presented them to me. So I used his leaves to make whistles one after another and gave them to him. Sounds of whistles, high and low, far and near, filled the air and aroused more nostalgia in me. Oh, the intimate small-fruited fig trees in my birthplace, it was in the bosom of your shade that I grew up. If you have perception, can you perceive that I am thinking of you in the far-away strange land? If you have thought, can you think of me like a mother, the man residing far from the birthplace?

Oh, the small-fruited fig trees in my birthplace⋯

The translator's notes:

About the author: Huang Helang (1941 – 2012) was born in Fujian Province of China. He lived in Hong Kong for 20 years and has been generally regarded as a Hong Kong poet and writer though he lived in Hawaii since 1995 and was the chair of the Chinese Writers' Association of Hawaii.

About the translation and the essay: The first mainland publication of this essay can be found in *Fujian Youth*, Issue 6, 1980. The title of this periodical was changed into *Youth Tide* in 1993. The translation was based on the edition of 100 *Essays during the* 60 *Years in China* published in 2009. In this essay, the author's recollection goes back to the time when he was still a small child. A lot of savory countryside scenes around the trees are vividly described in it.

Recollections of My Childhood

Liu Meng

The kaleidescope

My childhood, as far as I can remember, was dominated by some kind of dreariness.

I was born and raised in a small town in Northern China. Life there was so monotonous and dry that it was suffocating. Particularly for a child full of fantasy, the world was definitely too narrow and cramped. I never played different games from those played by earlier generations. Neither had I the least idea what it was like outside our hometown. It was through the mouth of some lucky pal of mine who had been to a big city that I learned that children of the city had a lot of wonderful toys and a great deal of fun. However, I could only imagine what the toys looked like and how they were played with and never dared to nurse the smallest hope of coming into the possession of them. At the time when I was small, except for a few substantial families, parents had to work very hard to eke out a living, to say nothing of buying toys for their children. Year in and year out, I never got hold of any plaything.

One winter, snow fell heavily for nights, covering every street and lane, and made it impossible for us children to play outside. Being unable to stay quietly at home, we jumped wildly all about on the *kang* (bed made of brick or mud brick—the translator) and on the floor. This really disturbed the adults, leaving them unable to have a rest or do any housework. To coax us to quiet down, Grandma said: "Be good. I'll make a nice plaything for you. " As children are always curious, we were as happy to have a toy as we would be to hear there was something good to eat. Immediately, we all sat aside without making any more noise.

Grandma happened to be very versatile. With strips of glass she made a triangular tube, wrapped it with cardboard to turn it into a cylinder, pasted some paper as the cover, and then put bits of glass and scraps of colored paper inside. After all of this, she sealed one end of it, and cut a small hole in the other. The toy was thus finished. While turning the tube, Grandma peeped into it for a long time. Then she passed it to me, but before letting it go, she asked in all seriousness: "Are you going to be naughty again?" With my hand already stretching out, I answered hastily: "Never again!" She chuckled and gave it to me: "Put it near one of your eyes, and look through the hole while turning it around. You'll see a lot of beautiful patterns. " I took it over and peered. Sure enough, every turn brought a new picture. How odd and interesting it was!

From then on, I had a toy of my own. I asked what the toy was called, and Grandma told me it was a kaleidoscope. In the company of it, I passed many unforgettable days. Even now, whenever memories of childhood come back to me, I recall the great pleasure the kaleidoscope gave me. It really adds a touch of warmth to my recollection of the primarily dreary childhood.

The lantern of cabbage

The Spring Festival at my home town was always enveloped in great jubilation. Every family would paste up colorful scissor-cuts on the windows or doors and some families even struck up antithetical couplets. "We must mark the end of the year with auspicious signs," the local people would say.

The festival meant something different to the children, whose concerns were great fun and good food. All through the holidays, the streets and lanes were full of laughter and the sound of firecrackers of the children. The whole world seemed to belong to them for the time being. On New Year's Eve, as soon as it was getting dark, all boys and girls, each with a lantern in hand, swarmed into the streets, and compared each other's lanterns for the brightest and prettiest. All kinds of lanterns made of paper or glass, bought from the country fair or simply homemade, dotted the dark night like stars. It was an exceptional sight, especially when being viewed from a distance.

At one Spring Festival, much to my delight, Father bought me a square glass lantern with some goldfish painted on it. Early on that New Year's Eve, I excitedly lit the lantern and went outside holding it. Seeing some children already there comparing their lanterns, I hurried my pace to join them. Yet before I reached them I tripped and fell and broke the glass lantern. Very disappointedly, I returned home and cried for a similar one. However, with every shop and fair already closed for the festival, there was simply nowhere for us to buy another. Disturbed by my great bitterness, Grandma, who was preparing dumplings, the traditional food for New Year's Eve with other adults of the family, caught sight of the cabbages on the chopping board and hit on an idea.

"Stop crying, boy," Grandma said. "According to the old saying, you'll be safe year after year. (In Chinese, "break" and "year" happen to be pronounced the same as "sui. " And there was an old saying "sui sui ping an" meaning "safe year after year. "—the translator.) Now let me make a nice novel cabbage lantern for you. " With that, she plucked a few outer leaves of a cabbage, chopped them into pieces of the same size and stood them in a circle, which was fixed with an iron wire. Then the circle, just as good as a lantern cover, was put on the holder of the candle retrieved from the broken lantern. With the small red candle inside lit again, it was very exceptional to see the swaying little fire encased in the white and green cabbage leaves, which gave out some dim light. When I finally joined the other children, they took the lantern as a special design. While looking at it admiringly, everyone exclaimed at its prettiness.

This unexpected but interesting episode of childhood has since remained in my memory. Whenever I see any lantern during the festivals, I think of the cabbage lantern. Its simple and unadorned cabbage-leaf cover and little red candle fire have always worked as a comfort for my heart which has still preserved some childlike innocence and made me think that I am not so advanced in years as I really am.

The promise

When I was small, I was frequently afflicted with diseases.

As the eldest grandchild of the family, I got the dearest love from Grandma. For fear that one day a serious disease might take my life, Grandma, who was illiterate, talked over the matter with my mother: if I could pass through my ten-year's birthday safe and sound, they should prepare a paper saddle[1] to be contributed to the Goddess when we paid religious homage to her in the first month of the lunar year.

Interestingly enough, when I was ten, I started to become much stronger. Grandma and Mother, both of whom had never stepped out of the

neighborhood, believed that it was the Goddess that acted upon the improvement of my health. As they were honest and kind-hearted women,
they were now determined to have the promise they made between themselves fulfilled. My family was by no means well-off at that time. Besides,
not being the head of the family, neither of them could draw any extra
money from the family's limited resources. It was not easy for them to manage to have a paper saddle made. For some time, they cut down the expenses for food and clothes to save the money, in addition to borrowing here
and there. When they finally had enough, they ordered a paper saddle in
the county town. As I remember clearly, it was a beautiful saddle made
from a great variety of color paper, much similar to a real one in shape and
size.

One day in the first month of the Chinese lunar year, led by Grandma, I carried the saddle on my back and stood in the long line of the children waiting to kowtow before the statue of the Goddess in the temple to re-
deem vows. However, we children were only children. When we looked at
each other, we could feel nothing but some laughable fun. The pious a-
dults, unable to stand such irreverence, kept rebuking or wheedling the
children, as if handling some untamed ponies.

When my turn came, I kowtowed and put the paper saddle into the
flaming fire according to the routine of such a ceremony. [2] I then felt a great
relief as if I had finished the homework assigned by the teacher. As for
Grandma, she was obviously overwhelmed with joy. Her hearty content-
ment could be easily observed from the smile on her face, which I had seldom seen.

Now, whenever I've recalled this incident, I have had a recurring so-
licitude: it was fortunate that my grandma and mother only promised a pa-

per saddle to the Goddess. If they had promised a true one, how could they have been able to manage it?

The ferrying

The small town where I was born and bred is located in the plain of east Hebei Province. It was said that the town was among the hardest hit when Tangshan had that earthquake in 1976. All the houses, streets and lanes of the town as I can remember were reduced to debris that time. Only the Ji Canal, which nurtures the local people, flows peacefully, free from any care.

It is still delightful for me to recall how we children spent the hot summer days swimming in the canal and catching birds with nets in the forest of reeds years ago. Yet children could seldom concentrate on the same activities over and over again. When we were bored with swimming and birdcatching, we would beg the ferryman for a free ride in order to play on the other side of the canal.

At that time, the ferry must be paid. So our begging often met with firm refusal.

However, there was a ferryman called Uncle Shuan, who was very fond of children and liked playing with us. As a result, few of the children feared him. Whenever it was Uncle Shuan's turn to take charge of the ferry, we would say good words to him and help him with some chores, and he, in turn, would gladly let us get on board and give us one or two free rides. Sometimes, when he was happy, he would allow us several free rides. If one of us added: "Uncle Shuan, my father invites you to have a drink of wine at my home when you get off the ferry boat," he would be in even higher spirits: "Boys, let me sing you a song." Then the hoarse voice began to ring over the limpid canal:

Firmly I stand at the stern rocking the scull,

Further and further we are rocking into the canal...

Both the notes and the words of the song were difficult for us. It was when growing up that we came to understand the words. What we felt at that time was only a kind of sheer fun.

When we were tired of playing on board, we would make faces to each other and jump into the river one by one. Once, someone even shouted out to Uncle Shuan: "Nobody invited you to have a drink of wine, they just want you to have a drink of urine!" But Uncle Shuan did not get angry with this. He simply smiled good-naturedly and said: "Bad chaps. You can't expect me to let you come on board next time." However, when the next time actually came, he again allowed us to play on board.

The wrestling

As a place standing on the bank of the river, facing the sea further on the east, close to Tianjin and Tangshan, and with a railroad running through on one side of it, my hometown should have been a busy and lively seat. Yet, in my memory, it seemed to be a girl living in the mountains or in a deep and secluded valley, who had fine and delicate looks, but was not vivacious in character. The children in the town had mostly lived in dreariness and rarely had anything interesting or delightful to do. An occasional monkey show or sugar-man-making put on by mobile actors or peddlers would draw all children in and around the neighborhood. Heated and noisy talks about the performance they saw would last several days on end.

But I don't mean to say that there were not any other diversions. Boys and girls there often played games, such as hopscotch, rope-skipping, hide-and-seek, shuttlecock kicking, etc. , which might have been passed to us from primitive generations. Nothing but wrestling seemed to belong to boys of spirited and resolute disposition. Girls could just watch such a game, but never dared to take part in it.

Naughty boys, whenever they felt like it, would give an open challenge to each other, and in a minute would cross their arms together, each staring at his rival and thinking hard how to use his legs efficiently. Usually they were at once surrounded by a crowd of children and in the shouts of the onlookers the little wrestlers tried their best to outdo the other. My neighbor had a boy called Big Pillar. He was both strong and agile, and could easily beat, one by one, several opponents. As he was always the winner in wrestling matches, he had won everybody's admiration. Later, some shameful performance of his made the children keep clear of him.

One day a boy from another village came to see the wrestling. After Big Pillar had pinned three others, the boy offered to have a match with him. Seeing he was only a lean child one head shorter than himself, Big Pillar took up the challenge right away. At first he proceeded carelessly, thinking he was bound to win. When he was unexpectedly thrown down by the small challenger, he refused to admit defeat. So instead of trying again to get the better of the opponent, he bit the boy in the shoulder. With a cry, the boy let go of him. This made the children of our neighborhood feel some kind of disgrace. As to Big Pillar, he was seldom seen playing wrestling again...

The snow

Winter, in my memory, was always connected with cold and snow. For me, without the two, winter cannot be called winter. Hence, in this coldest third nine-day period after the winter solstice, I naturally recall a story of snow.

When I was small, one winter was just like that of Beijing this year—

no snow even when the winter reached the coldest period. The local people were very worried. Whenever they met each other, "snow" seemed to be the sole topic: "If there is no snow soon, people will fall ill. " "No snow now, no good harvest the next year. Then what shall we live on?" All their words and worrying looks remain fresh in my memory. The difference is that I can understand better their state of mind now than I could then.

There was a geomancer who told the anxious and eager locals: "Let's make a snowman and beg for snow. " My poor and ignorant folks accepted his suggestion without any question, though they had only begged for rain before and did not know whether snow could also be begged or not. They at once set about making a number of snowmen with faggots and white paper. Then they burned joss sticks, laid offerings before the snowmen and piously begged the Heaven, which they thought dictated rain and snow, to bestow upon them a favor. With all of the begging and praying going on, one day, two days, ⋯ fifteen days passed, and there was no sign of snow. The local folks were bitterly disappointed and began to curse their own fate.

Just as the local people were in great despair, a strong wind brought about a heavy fall of snow, which blotted out the sky and covered up every spot of the earth. It fell continuously for one day and one night. Everybody grinned from ear to ear. "Good snow, good snow," were the first words they exchanged when they saw each other. The children were happier: they chased one another, rolled about in the snow, built up snowmen, and threw snowballs at each other. They also sang cheerfully from time to time: "When the snow is falling and covers the road, there's no worry of food and wood. " It seemed as if this fall of snow would really help the local people shake off their poverty. We children, knowing nothing about natural sciences, merely argued about whether the snow fell as a result of the geomancer's prayers. Some said "yes" and some said "no. " Nobody could ever convince his antagonist or tell how and why. The one thing we all a-greed with was that the fall of snow was good. As to the reasons, one child said: "My grandma told me snow can kill disease-inducing little things and prevent people from falling ill. " Another voice then rose: "My father said heavy snow is good for crops. And we'll have enough to eat. " In a word, all wished for a good life.

This is the children's snow day or the snow day's children in my mem-ory. The snow is pure, so are the children. The pity is that though we can have snowy days again, we'll never have another childhood.

The translator's notes:

1. It was believed that the gods and goddesses rode imaginary horses, so the local people would promise that if the child could get well, they would rather let the child become a horse to be ridden by the goddess. Pre-paring a saddle for the child to carry when he was asked to thank the god-dess symbolized the child's becoming a horse. Moreover, in Chinese the word for saddle (an) is a homophone of the Chinese character meaning "safe" or "healthy".

2. According to the relevant Chinese tradition, the recovered child was asked to carry the paper saddle when coming to fulfill the promise in order to beg the goddess to accept him or her as a horse. When the paper saddle was burned, it was believed that the ash of it, while containing this will, could go with the wind up into the sky and reach the goddess.

About the author: Liu Meng (1935 -) is a senior editor of the Chi-nese Writers' Association and a well-known writer, who has published a number of collections of essays.

About the essay: This essay was a collection of short pieces written in different years of 1980s. Apart from childhood disappointment and pleasure in the traditional activity of comparing each other's lantern during the Spring Festival mentioned in the second piece "The lantern of cabbage", the author is kind of critical of the old women's practice of wasting money on superstition in the 1940s in "The promise", and reveals some children's anti-traditional behavior—not respecting the elder and this simple ferryman's generosity and tolerance in "The ferrying". The last second piece reflected the traditional Chinese moral standard about what is right and what is wrong in a wrestling. In the last one the author shows his nostalgic feelings about the purity of the countryside children as well as a touch of criticism about the elder folks' superstition that snow or rain could be begged for by offerings in the 1940s when he was still a child.

The Nine-Curve Turning

Liu Chengzhang

Treading on the thin layer of snow, I arrived at the Zhao Family Gully.

This was a village more than forty kilometers away from the Yan'an city. Though only middle-sized, it had recently built dozens of stone cave dwellings which appeared to be an orderly pile of gray from a distance. Windows and doors of the new cave dwellings were all strong and bright, with red couplets and paper-cuts pasted on them. Like the aroma from a jar of good wine, the abundance of life, the animation of the Spring Festival, and the happiness of the people wafted directly to my lungs.

On the school sports ground, cleared of snow, in front of the village, a group of neatly-dressed men was busy digging small pits to erect sorghum stems. I knew even without inquiring that they were making preparations for the nine-curve turning. I had specially come to watch this activity.

According to some legends, the nine-curve turning was also called the Yellow River battle formation of nine curves that had been practiced in ancient wars. Later, it became a folk custom in northern Shaanxi Province to display colorfully decorated lanterns in the same formation at Spring Festivals so that people could wander about and enjoy themselves among the lanterns turning many curves. This was just what we now called the nine-curve turning. Although my afterbirth had been buried on the bank of the Yanhe River and I grew up by drinking water from this river, I never got a chance to see this ceremony. Who could be in a mood to observe this custom in the chaos of the previous years? With the sharp increase of agricultural output in this area, people began to live a satisfactory life and the ancient folk custom to celebrate the festival had therefore been revived. This custom had been restored both in cities and in the countryside. After years of writing, I preferred the countryside scenes to the city ones, so I had come all the way here from the capital of the province to seek for what one could also enjoy in the city.

While talking to each other, the villagers and I got more and more familiar and did not shun any subjects. Later, I heard them making a joke with a young man, who had long hair on the temples. I wondered how the hair style popular in the present southern cities should be seen in this remote gully. An old man called Uncle Yang was teasing the "Long Hair:"

"Hi, Fellow. To call you a man, but your hair is too long for that; to call you a woman, but you have no braids!"

These words evoked a roar of laughter. Also laughing, "Long Hair" began to twist the arm of a plump young man, who hastened to run around the other people to dodge. Looking at them I found the "Long Hair" was also a simple and likable young man.

The powerfully-built leader of the production team, just in his thirties, was laughing with the others till all became quiet. Then he took on a serious look and said to the "Long Hair:"

"Go quickly and have a haircut! Now I'd like to make clear beforehand that if you don't, you won't be allowed to take part in the nine-curve turning activity. ”

"Long Hair" turned his head away in an unconvinced way, but he also blushed and just dug pits on the ground without a word.

I had noticed from the beginning that they were erecting the sorghum stems upside-down. The hairy roots of the sorghum, each having been trimmed, now served as the tops. I asked the team leader why they were so put, and he answered:

"Each sorghum stem should support one lantern. ”

I had guessed the sorghum stem must be used as posts for lanterns.

"It is only on the trimmed roots turning upward that the lanterns could be steadily put. ”

How stupid I was to have supposed that the lanterns would be hung with thin ropes on the sorghum stems. If I had not seen it in person, how could I have had some idea of all of this?

Seeing I was more or less tired with walking, the team leader quitted his work and led me to the village to have a rest in a quiet public cave dwelling. About one hour later, I heard that some women were making the lanterns in a nearby cave dwelling, so I hurried to go up there to have a look.

The sound of chatting and laughing of women could be heard from far away. When I entered I saw all girls and young married women there were very busy. Some were making the lantern cups, some, the lantern rafts, and some, the lantern covers. The cups were made of potatoes chopped in square, round or pentagonal shapes with a hole dug in the center of each one. The thin top ends of sorghum where the grain had grown were used to make the rafts. They were halved and cut into one-inch pieces. Then two pieces were tied together to form a little cross. On the point of the intersection was put the wick of the lantern. When the lantern was used, the raft would be floating on the oil in the cup. As to the lantern covers, they were made of pretty red or green paper.

I was greatly surprised by the village women's wonderful workmanship. Every lantern they made could have been sent to an exhibit of arts and crafts. I could not help complimenting them. Then a silver voice was heard:

"As hemp blossoms appear in circles, you make such a detour to laugh at us!"

This was the response from one of the young girls. To my great surprise, what she offhandedly said was similar to the device of the folk tune called Xintianyou[1], popular in northern Shaanxi, and her tone sounded like piano playing. I then paid more attention to her and found she was an oval-faced, rosy-cheeked girl dressed in a red cotton-padded jacket, and she looked very clever, especially about the eyes and brows. According to her accent, she must have come from the area around Suide County and Mizhi County in northern Shaanxi.

"How can I laugh at you since I could never learn your craft no matter how hard I tried," said I.

"You really flattered me too much," said the girl with a stroke of her hair. "Not another woman is more awkward than I in the whole gully. If you want to see the most masterly woman, go to the neighboring cave."

As told by the others, the young girl's name was Yeye.

Just at that time, the lattice of the window was hit by a little piece of stone. All of the women burst into laughter, only Yeye lowered her head. A married woman who was chopping a lantern cup said with a smile:

"Be quick to get out, Yeye, in case he becomes impatient with waiting. ”

"Let him wait even if he is impatient to death!" Yeye answered with a blushed face.

I already guessed who it could be that was calling her. But I was not familiar enough with her to make a joke, so I just went away to see the most skilled woman.

The most admired " masterly woman" turned out to be a wrinkled grandma sitting among a group of women in the next cave dwelling. She was clipping the paper-cuts for the big lanterns. I was amazed to see that without any ready design, she could cut within twenty minutes forty or fifty lifelike figures, each with a different face, doing the *yangko*, a popular local folk dance. The other women told me that she was even asked to demonstrate her paper-cutting before Chairman Mao (president of China from 1949 to 1976—the translator) when she was young.

Although I was still not quite sure about how the nine curves were turned, the preparations for this activity already filled my mind with excitement.

After supper, it began to snow. The snowflakes were tiny and thin. In the air, the appeal of the snow was mixed with the delicious whiffs of fried cakes, malt sugar and millet wine. Also merged in the mixture was the incessant sound of chatting and laughing heard during the whole day, which now became louder. Then suddenly rose the sound of gongs and drums accompanied by the *suona* horn, the traditional Chinese woodwind instrument. At the same time, dogs, black and white, began to bark competitively before their owners' homes. Men and women, old and young, swarmed to the school sports ground with the *yangko* team—it was time for the nine-curve turning!

Mingled in the crowd, I was walking with the leader of the production team. Snowflakes fell on my face and made me feel cool and itching. A child, in his hurry to run forward, almost tripped me. The team leader supported me in time, then scolded the child and told me to walk more slowly and be more careful. However, he himself strode ahead more and more quickly and later he pulled my hand and broke into a run. I knew it was because this was the first time to restore the custom in this village after many years, and he wanted to arrive on the spot earlier to ensure that everything was in order. I ran with him in high spirits, for I was quite used to running in the mountains from early childhood. It was really a great pleasure to be among the first ones to watch the scene.

Before us, the lanterns that turned nine curves were shining brightly. Like stars, their radiant rays lit up the mountain gully with the snowflakes floating all through the sky. I felt as if I had seen such a spectacle before. Then I remembered it had been the day following the National Day last year when I flew from Beijing to Xi'an and looked at the thousands of twinkling lights of Xi'an city. It was quite similar to this, but only on a much bigger scale. The scene of this evening could be said to be the miniature of what I saw on the plane over Xi'an. However, this day's lights were arranged much more orderly, forming lines vertically and horizontally. In addition, the myriads of snowflakes in haloes of light made it a much more intoxicating sight of glistening haziness.

Approaching, I saw ten big lanterns hanging high around the sports ground, each with part of the paper-cut in the shape of a *yangko* team clipped by the old skilled woman pasted on. Suddenly, the sports ground was full of people dancing and waving the colorful silk bands. Did the *yangko* team jump down from the lanterns?

To the sound of gongs, drums and *suona* horns, the *yangko* team, led by a guide holding a fancy umbrella, first entered the meandering lantern array. Accompanied by the rhythms of the gongs and drums, the guide was turning up and down the umbrella, which now looked very much like whirl-pools in the curving Yellow River. The colorful silk bands waving inces-santly by each member of the *yangko* team seemed to be the bright colored clouds sailing over the river. About the revolving umbrella snowflakes were whirling shiningly; with the waving of the silk bands, snowflakes flew up glisteningly. All was moving in endless circles in the blaze of lantern lights: the umbrella in beautiful design, the colorful silk bands, the shin-ing snowflakes, and the smiling faces...

The graceful and flowing dancing of the *yangko* team put me in a daz-zled and surprised admiration. I had worked in a professional troupe for many years and was quite familiar with a great number of actors and actres-ses, some of whom were really quite accomplished in the arts, but none of them could perform with such zeal. Even the lively figures in the skilled woman's paper-cut would have had a sense of inferiority. I imagined the *yangko* team now turning and dancing in the lanterns arranged in nine curves to be a huge paper-cut, clipped by an immense pair of scissors of tradition and reality and pasted on the gigantic lantern of good life.

With the masses in lines, I entered the lantern curves, too. It looked as if all the bright light in the world was collected here. The lanterns, the eyes, the smiling faces, even the wind that blew gently, were shining. The swirling snowflakes in shining haloes resembled small lights flying in the air. I saw in the luminous rows of people old men and women, and mothers with their children all glowing brightly. Almost all of the villagers had come: the oldest was eighty-nine and the youngest were those who had just learned to walk. Everybody, radiant and smiling, was turning the curves joyfully with gentle steps treading on the snow to the rhythms of the drums.

I felt my mind also became luminous with the rising of a colorful rainbow of imagination. How the lanterns appeared like blossoming flowers and the people like flying butterflies with fluttering shining wings around them. The lanterns also bore some resemblance to the ripe sorghum, and the people seemed to be holding shining sickles and singing resonant songs. The lanterns in orderly lines were somehow similar to the music staff of a wonderful movement or quivering violin strings and the people the music notes rising and falling between them...

Suddenly there arose a roar of laughter and everyone looked at the spot behind me. I hurried to turn around and found that Uncle Yang who had followed me closely now began to dance *yangko* with snowflakes shaken off him. His artistic gestures revealed him to be a good hand at this dance, but to amuse the people, he was overacting. I waited till he had enjoyed himself to the full.

"Uncle, how old are you?" I asked.

"Sixteen," he answered with a laugh. Rays of light came off his brows, reflecting of a few snowflakes.

"He's sixty," the team leader explained. "When he was small, Comrade Zhou Enlai (the first premier of P. R. China—the translator) once taught him to read and write. "

"How lucky you were!" Looking at Uncle Yang, I tried to raise my voice above the sound of gongs and drums. At the same time, a ray of light drifted into one of my eyes and a few snowflakes entered my mouth.

"I was happy then and now. As the years in between," Uncle Yang said with a sigh, "I could find no happiness but the beggar's stick!" He continued after a pause: "It's not good to recollect those days. I only want you to know that last year, I alone had a harvest of eight thousand *jin* (half a kilogram—the translator) of grain!"

With overflowing happiness, he hoped that I could tell those who had worked in Yan'an to come back and see with their own eyes that Yan'an was again as prosperous as the period when the Great Production Movement was carried out during the 1940's under the leadership of the Central Committee of the Chinese Communist Party then located there, and that everybody had enough to eat and wear and was full of happiness. The dark recollection was only a fleeting thought; all was so bright before us.

Then I remembered "Long Hair," who had not been seen about. A little disconsolately, I slightly poked the team leader walking before me and blamed him for giving the severe order to that young man and thus preventing him from taking part in the revelries. The team leader pointed to the left of us:

"What's that? There he comes!"

I looked at that direction carefully and found him beyond lines of lanterns. This time his hair style was exactly similar to that of the other young men. Clearly he had already had a haircut. Who was the girl in front of him, that was so intimate with him? The girl turned around smilingly and gave him a handful of something, which he swallowed up happily with the snowflakes and the light. At last I recognized that the girl was Yeye.

"A couple of lovers," the team leader said. "It was actually Yeye who did not like his long hair. The girl once declared seriously that if he continued to have long hair, she would break off her relationship with him! Why, didn't I give the order to help him?"

The team leader's voice seemed shiny, too. Illuminated by the lanterns arranged in the nine curves, everything was harmonious, substantial and enchanting. I felt I was lingering with the simple and honest country folk in the glowing lines of a poem.

It began to snow more heavily and flakes fell thick and fast. The haloes about the flakes were whirling bigger. The heads, brows and shoulders of people were covered with glistening snow; all looked like jade sculptures. The heavier snow made the people more excited and they turned more enthusiastically in the light and snowflakes.

We passed one lantern after another, each standing for one day. There were altogether three hundred sixty-five lanterns symbolizing the whole year. I blessed the people and wished that every day would be bright for them.

More lanterns were passed by. The meandering lanterns reminded us of our road forward. The road we had just covered was tortuous, the road we were going to cover was also tortuous. However, on the tortuous road or at whatever place we might meet with hardship and difficulties, we would be guided by the light like this night and never lose heart. Even if we might drop a few tears of sorrow sometimes, the light of hope would be contained in them.

Still more lanterns were passed by. With thoughts thronging my mind, I withdrew from the festive sports ground.

How I felt regret at parting from all this! Looking back, I wanted to reenter it and take some light with me as if it were a poem or a handkerchief given by my love when we had first fallen in love. I believed the pieces of light would shine in the cave dwellings of all families and bring them, old or young, a transparent and sweet dream.

The translator's notes:

1. The device of Xintianyou mainly consists of pairs of antithetical phrases, clauses or sentences, with the first one being a simile or metaphor.

About the author: Liu Chengzhang (1937 –) is a notable poet, essayist and has published quite a number of collections of essays. Many of his lyrical essays focus on Shaanxi Province of China, especially on Northern Shaanxi.

About the essay: This essay was published in *Essays*, Issue 10, 1982. As that time was just the beginning of China's opening-up, people tended to reexamine the past years with critical eyes and enjoyed the newest policies in every aspect, say, culture, agriculture, etc. However, people in remote inland areas still could not accept some changes, say, some new style of hair though such things were already common in south of China, the pioneer in China's opening-up.

The Fire Gourds

Liu Chengzhang

Xi'an, a city with the red swaying and the green spilling most of the year, seems always to be transformed into a huge mass of gray in winter. Despite the young people's stubborn perseverance in making a display of their juvenile vigor by wearing a sky-blue overcoat one day and a multi-colored shawl on the other, all is only too weak to outdo the dominant gray, which envelops everything, making the youth's brightness a mere passing flash.

When the northwest wind is blowing, dust coats the Bell Tower, originally in splendid green and gold, and turns it into a looming gray pile. It requires great effort to make out a trace of its resplendence.

The gray naturally reminds people of the countless historical relics excavated around Xi'an. As the capital of eleven ancient dynasties, Xi'an is full of rare treasures. It is said that whenever you drop in at a farmer's house near Xi'an and casually pick up a piece of pottery or even a fragment of tile, you will discover very frequently that it is a historical relic, if identified by a specialist. With the winter's devouring gray, the whole city looks like an immense historical relic just unearthed.

For days on my way to and from work, I saw the city bustling and flourishing: all kinds of dresses, suits and trousers on sale were hung high, fluttering and swaying in the wind above the facades of shops; the then popular singer Zhu Mingying's sweet voice was heard flowing from the double-cassette tape recorders; delicious smells kept entering your nostrils, coming from the restaurants serving *yangroupao*—a stew of mutton and minced unleavened pancakes; here and there spread on the pavement for sale were scraping cutters for peeling potatoes, newly-written novels on martial arts and chivalrous deeds, and glue for catching mice as they would stick to where the glue was applied. Among the automobiles and bicycles busy coming and going in all directions, tricycles could now and then be seen moving slowly and cautiously bearing refrigerators or wardrobes of the newest design which had just been purchased. However, all these were not what I wanted to see or what I liked to see. In my mind's eye, they were also wrapped in gray. To watch them was just like seeing an endless and monotonous black-and-white film, which would soon make you bored and sleepy. A kind of hankering suddenly rose in my mind, though I could not tell what it was.

One morning I went to the provincial government in the center of the city to attend a meeting. Owing to the recent snow, the air was pure and fresh while the sun illuminated brightly. When reaching the middle part of the Northern Avenue, I saw in front of my eyes something in burning red, which greatly buoyed up my spirits. With a second look, I found it was a bicycle carrying high at the back an enormous bunch of scores of tiny red lanterns, closely clustered together. The man who rode on the bicycle was obviously a farmer. The man, the bicycle and the lantern bunch constituted a perfect image of a gigantic squirrel. The lantern bunch, large, bright-colored, and rising high, looked very much like the tail of the squirrel, whose brisk life was vividly embodied by the farmer who was busy pedaling ahead.

I found it hard to resume my journey right away. It acted on me like hearing the thundering sound of drums and gongs when I just emerged from a silent jungle. I felt extremely satisfied. And now I began to know what it was that I had longed for.

Nevertheless, when I looked again, the squirrel disappeared in the twinkling of an eye, leaving me there relishing the aftertaste.

For a few days after that, whenever walking on the street, I searched keenly for the squirrel and the burning red, yet all I saw was the moving and jostling crowds. I walked silently, wondering why the color of the lanterns was so bright and how they looked like balls of fire coming from the depths of the earth.

Finally I saw the squirrel with the large, rising tail of vivid red again. There were more squirrels than just one: three or four. From then on, everyday more and more such squirrels appeared. Each sight of them would make me feel very delighted and become conscious that the Spring Festival and the closely following Lantern Festival were approaching.

The display of lanterns on the 15th day of the first lunar month is an ancient custom, said to date from the Han Dynasty (206 B. C. – 220 A. D.) and became most popular and grand in the Tang Dynasty (618 – 907 A. D.). During that time a hundred of lantern trees almost as tall as 90 feet or colossal wheels bearing fifty thousand lanterns were made for each festival, magnificently illuminating the entire capital of the country then—the present Xi'an. Today a great variety of festive lanterns, modern or traditional, simple or refined, can still be seen in the city. Among the traditional folk lanterns, the most well-known are the sheep lanterns of the

Dongcang Alley, the rabbit lanterns of the Zhou Family Alley, the five-lo-
tus-flower lanterns of the Li Family Village, the lion lanterns of the Bean-
curd Alley..., especially the lanterns called "fire gourds" turned out in
Baqiao—Ba Bridge. The number of the fire gourds is overwhelming of all
the festive lanterns. The above-mentioned squirrel tails rising high are just
clusters of fire gourds.

I loved fire gourds as well as the squirrel tails consisting of them,
moving from one place to another in the streets of Xi'an. To me, it was a
great spiritual comfort to see the open, vivid, and poetic red.

Later I got a chance to have a close examination of the red squirrel
tail. It was found that two great poles leaning backwards were tied respectively on each side of the rear frame of the bicycle, and many thin twigs,
with fire gourds hanging in clusters on them, were fastened to the poles. In
fact, the fire gourds were not purely red, but with the two ends decorated
with green fancy borders and a golden tassel attached under each one. I
stood meditating on the fact that instead of weakening the red color, they
made the red more intense and conspicuous. Clearly the folk handicrafts-
men had a good sense of aesthetic dialectics.

I observed a cadre-like couple choosing a fire gourd for the child they
took, who obviously had just learned to walk. As soon as the lantern was
bought, the child eagerly snatched it, with sparkles in the eyes and dim-
ples on the cheeks, which manifested hearty satisfaction.

During the fortnight between the Spring Festival and the Lantern Festival, squirrels with the fire gourds, moving or standing, appeared in every
street and alley, inside and outside the inner city wall of Xi'an. There
seemed a sea of fire gourds, each of them was a lively folk tune produced
by the traditional Chinese wind and percussion instruments, giving off a

cataract of intense emotions. On the night of the Lantern Festival, it seemed as if the thousands of fire gourds had developed wings and all flown on the south side of the city wall. The dazzling and grand spectacle would have melted the iron or steel men among the spectators.

It is actually owing to this that the tender leaves of the willows and fresh bursting of all flowers cannot raise a ripple of excitement in my mind.

Oh, the most stirring fire gourds!

The translator's notes:

About the author: Liu Chengzhang (1937 –) is a notable poet, essayist and has published quite a number of collections of essays. Many of his lyrical essays focus on Shaanxi Province of China, especially on Northern Shaanxi.

About the essay: This essay was written at the end of 1985, which was just the year when people were very zealous about restoring the traditional customs after the Cultural Revolution (1966 – 1976) kept under restraint this kind of things.

Yulin—A City in Northern Shaanxi

Liu Chengzhang

Looking out of the long-distance bus, I, as one of the travelers saw beyond the vast valley to the west, where the rolling hills were covered with snow-like white sand. This vista provoked in me a sense of awe, reminding me that the winds had existed from time memorial down to the present day; all the force and form of the winds seemed to have been sculptured in the sand.

One by one the willow trees flashed by outside the bus. They were not the kind called Ba Willow, nor were they the supple twigs described in the Tang Dynasty (618 – 907) poems as parting presents, but merely the thick tree-trunks or severed thick branches, the thinner ones having been sawed off to make rafters. As it was not the season for putting out fresh leaves, they looked as if dark ink had been poured all over them, each resembling a black man's arm stretching toward the sky.

Now and then some small sand dunes would swing into my sight on both sides of the road. Small and rare as they were, they attracted my attention, for they made the scenery very different from what can be seen elsewhere. If we travelers wanted to see sights and savor the poetic touch of Yulin, this scene could serve as the emblem of the city and the theme of a poem on Yulin. Like lines of children sent to greet all the travelers by the welcoming Yulin people, the sand dunes seemed to compete with each other by shouting and pointing: "Here is Yulin, the ancient frontier city!"

No stranger ever could guess that at the foot of the deserted Great Wall there could be such an exquisite and beautiful little city with the old-fashioned *siheyuan*—compounds with houses reared in an orderly manner around the square courtyards, with the Bell Tower, and the Soaring Tower, and the Ten-thousand-Buddha Tower and then, some modern buildings. In the market, household appliances of superior quality were sold in department stores; and there were golden cakes with dates, copper kettles, aluminum pots, and vary-shaped spoons spread on the brick ground by the humbler peddlers to tempt the passersby. Looking dazzlingly golden and colorful was the Xingming Tower with its upturned eaves and tinkling windbells, which was built during the Ming Dynasty (1368 – 1644) and freshly renovated. For the moment only a breeze could be felt but not a grain of sand was stirred. The sky was transparently blue and the clouds were pure, dazzling white, rarely to be found and enjoyed over big cities. Thus, we travelers were generously embraced by Yulin even before showing our I. D. cards.

Oh, the enchanting Yulin city with its entirely different scenery! Oh, the place sung and praised by countless poets throughout history!

Yulin has been an all-inclusive city harboring friendly local citizens and generals who were posted to garrison this frontier and the relegated officials, mostly non-natives, in the old times. All through the years in Yulin there were Beijing people who introduced *siheyuan*, and Nanjing people who integrated the southern music with the northern Shaanxi folk tunes. As Shaanxi Province has been bounded by the present Inner Mongolian Auton-

omous Region on the north, traces of Mongolian culture are observed everywhere on account of this city's frequent and intimate contacts with the Mon-
gols. Influences of two other neighboring provinces—Ningxia to the northwest and Shanxi to the northeast of Shaanxi Province can also be seen. Owing to the long-established intercourse and intermarriage between people
from south, east, north and west, and the nourishment of the unique
peach-flower water, people in Yulin, male or female, are not only intelli-
gent, but also excessively handsome. This fact has long been reflected in a
northern Shaanxi folk saying: "Handsome as matrons of Mizhi and men of
Suide, none can match women of Yulin. " They are the prettiest of the
pretty. Even the famous singers or dance stars can hardly be better than
Yulin women, who, with thin waists, long legs and high breasts, are most
delicately fair-complexioned. What is more, some, if not all, of the winners of the Hong Kong beauty competition each year would be sweating all
over and feel burning hot to the undersides of the arches of their feet, much
inclined to hide themselves in the rat burrows if compared with the Yulin
women. The only aspects in which the Yulin women may appear a little inferior are that they do not use cosmetics and are often too simple to play the
coquette or act vain, according to the Yulin men, who take great pride in
their women. Indeed, these are not exaggerations. Once you make a tour
around Yulin city, you can see for yourself what charming complexions and
figures the Yulin women have. In some words of the Beijing language still
used by the local grannies, the Yulin women are best described as bright,
juicy, dainty and beautiful.

Conscious of their own prettiness, the Yulin women usually pay special attention to their clothing and appearance. When going out, they like
wearing colorful overcoats, tight cotton-padded jackets made from red silk

dotted with golden flowers, or fashionable, bright woolen sweaters, which make their high breasts more conspicuous. In addition, they wear well-ironed trousers of woolen fabric and walk around on shiny high-heeled leather shoes. Moreover, they usually have silk bows fastened to their hair. Some look even more charming by dressing their hair into a one-sided braid resting on one of their high breasts. Such graceful bearing of the braid can seldom be seen elsewhere; the Yulin women have a patent on this original display of female charm. Some of the travelers could not help but comment jocosely: It is in the Yulin women's attractive way of dressing their hair that oriental beauty really lies.

Yulin is usually windy and dusty. Whenever the sand is blown by the wind, the women are covered from top to toe with dust. Nevertheless, as soon as the wind stops, they all wash themselves clean and change their clothes immediately, as if by prior agreement, and reappear fresh and lovely.

The Yulin women are also blessed with beautiful voices. The atmosphere can be greatly enlivened by their musical voices where they are found speaking.

Although it is a little peculiar in a city that is located on the fringe of the desert, there are a few lotus-flower ponds, which seem to be especially meant for the women. Unfortunately for me, one of the travelers, it was not the season for lotus flowers to come into bloom producing a picturesque background for the Yulin women's superb prettiness. What a sight it is in the days when the flowers are in full blossom with slim and elegant women lingering around them!

To argue for the sake of arguing, someone would pick out a plain, dark-complexioned woman and say triumphantly: "See that! Not every woman in Yulin is pretty!" To this comment many would immediately retort: "Even the ten fingers don't have the same size. But why not calm down and calculate the percentage of the pretty women in all?" On hearing these words, people would be reminded of the fact that in other cities or towns of the nearby Guanzhong Plain in central Shaanxi, or at the luxury hotels of far-away Nanning city and Guangzhou city, girls worth looking back at are as few as stars at dawn. Now the person who deliberately argued to the contrary would withdraw his previous remark and speak highly of the good-looking Yulin women while regretting the inferior appearance of the women of his home town. Then added to all the praises and regrets, he would say: "Don't buy a return ticket for me, I'd rather live here all my life and die here!" This was certainly only a joke, for he was already over forty and loved his wife dearly.

Men of Yulin are generally humorous, straightforward and of martial bearing. Eating at the same table with an official of the local military subarea, many of the travelers noted the erect, disciplined poise and posture of a general. They were so impressed by his carriage that they said he should be sent to Beijing to be a foreign affair officer to represent the Chinese people's dignity. An entrepreneur of a village factory was seen to have a similar distinguished air. It was said that he had earned as much as one hundred thousand *yuan*. Once on his way to the White Cloud Mountain, he gave out as much as one thousand and two hundred to the old and sick he met with. At another time in the street his foot was trodden by a pedestrian from Ningxia, who was rather inarticulate. Before the Ningxia man managed an apology, the entrepreneur begged pardon first by saying: "I'm sorry for having put my foot under yours. "

A young man told us travelers that the men with whiskers often seen in the streets were all descendants of the Mongolians. However, before long we were told by other people that the facial features of this very young man were typical of the Mongolians, only he himself did not know that he, too, is a Mongolian. The revelation is really interesting. Everyone's blood lineage seems an enigma. However, it can be safely said that the Mongolian blood is flowing in the veins of most of the Yulin people.

Exactly like the Mongolians, the Yulin men are very fond of drinking. When walking in front of a restaurant or in the residential quarters, you would frequently hear the sound of the drinkers' finger-guessing game. Some would sing merrily while drinking and the singing would often be joined by their wives or other female members of the family, though they did not join in the drinking. People said that dead bodies were found each winter in the open air—those of drunkards who dropped to the ground on their way home after drinking too much in a relative's or a friend's house and who were then frozen to death.

The nickname of Yulin is the Camel City. In the past decades, Yulin men and camels were best friends to each other, but now camels can seldom be seen. Yet there stands in the city a large camel statue to remind people of the remote past. And in place of camels, motorcycles, the present favorite form of transportation for the Yulin people, are unexpectedly numerous—every few steps we travelers took, there was one motorcycle passing, as swift as the wind. Some people, though paying little attention to what they eat and wear—say, just an army cap on the head or a cloth belt to fasten the trousers—take pride in riding motorcycles, which is regarded as a fashion, a distinguished and admirable deed for which all the other things can be overlooked.

As a result, motorcycle repair shops have emerged in great numbers.

On the facade of each one, there is a sign indicating that both motors made in China and imported from foreign countries can be repaired. Clearly, the imported motors are widely enjoyed by the Yulin people.

Among the buildings in Yulin, the most appealing are the *siheyuan* compounds, most of which remain in good condition. Some such compounds, with newly-added houses to shelter the recently-born, appear rather crowded. Yet, in either case, their courtyards are paved with bricks and kept as clean as possible. It certainly is a characteristic of the Yulin people to keep everything clean. There are even some families that sweep their courtyards two or three times a day, hence the numerous broom sellers in the streets. Those brooms are all made from a kind of long, thin, and yellow grass, which looks fresh and cool.

Most of the *siheyuan* compounds are fronted with arches over the gateway, faced by screen walls with piles of shining coal before them. After entering a nearby house, you can see the coal burning well, always keeping the pots, big or small, boiling. You may even be told by an eighty-year-old man that high-quality coal has been found in great quantities around Yulin, Shenmu and Fugu. This area is estimated as one of the eight best coal mines in the world. It is said that the Japanese, the Americans and people from many other countries rushed over and suggested joint exploitations. However, as they always showed a tendency to profit at the local people's expense the negotiations did not come off and the Chinese people began to mine the coal themselves. The railway is already extended to Daliuta, close to Yulin. People believe that within a few years, Yulin will become a thriving scene of bustle and excitement. Already the newly-discovered coal has greatly excited the Yulin people, who talk endlessly about it.

The other thing that is often on the lips of the people is money. If discussions about the coal are local, then those about money are quite universal. Traveling around China, one can hear such discussions everywhere, on the planes or in the buses. Yulin is no exception. Since ancient times, Yulin has been a town more marked with a commercial atmosphere than other places. An ancient horse market found in the ruins in the north of the city serves as a good example of this aspect of Yulin. It would be strange if Yu Lin remained outside of the nation-wide "commercial rush". When neighbors living in the same *siheyuan* talk to each other, "money" is inevitably mentioned in the very first few words, like bedbugs crawling about or flies flying over the otherwise very clean courtyards. Even the Yulin people's pleasant voices are contaminated by this vulgar word.

Active in the wool trade are many men in their prime and girls in their twenties, but I, the traveler noticed that some of them often hid sand in their wool, or packed stinking shoes, old shorts or whatever odd heavy things they could find. When these degraded acts were noted, the elders would say cynically: "Why always accuse the foreigners of attempting to gain extra advantages by unfair means? What are our men and girls up to? What a wicked idea it is! " This kind of criticism was immediately confirmed by other elders who commented: "What do they expect but reimbursement being demanded by the cheated foreign businessmen when these crooked shipments of wool arrived in their countries? " On hearing these words, I could feel nothing but a little sick at heart while thinking of the flower-like pretty girls.

How I wished that this kind of thing would cease. For the moment I just tried to forget the depressing facts and went elsewhere to continue the sightseeing.

Outside of the *siheyuan* house compounds is a crisscross network of al-leys, which, straight and serene, are all paved with bricks. Some alleys are so narrow that only one person can pass at one time. It is these narrow trails that give Yulin a touch of exquisiteness. The fat and heavy may find it rather difficult to pass through the narrow alleys with ease, but fortunate-ly, seldom can a fat person be seen in Yulin. It seems that these alleys were especially designed for the numerous slender women, who sometimes meet head-on in the alleys, but with gurgles of delight, they can always a-void a collision just in time, as swift and spry as a swallow. Walking along the alleys, you may see now a red figure flash past a gateway, now a basin sprinkling some water from one door, now a wheel of a brand-new bicycle coming out of another—all can immediately remind you how many pretty women are hidden in the deep and serene alleys.

Much to some of the local people's delight, tall commercial buildings, grand guest houses and cinemas have appeared one after another in Yulin, which is becoming more and more magnificent daily. Nevertheless, other people often feel it a pity that many *siheyuan* house compounds have been pulled down to make way for the new buildings, thus making the city lose some of its antique touch. We travelers all asked the same question in our minds: Why should people demolish the traditional buildings still in good condition, when, instead, the builders could make use of the vast barren land around the city? The builders seemed also conscious of this loss and deliberately gave some new buildings a look of primitive simplicity. The most conspicuous sight was the bright red couplets on the two sides of the doors and the windows leading to the open balconies of the new residential buildings of light green. In the newly-paved streets fresh advertisements could be seen here and there, such as the ads for a ten-day tour from Yulin

157

to Beijing, or those for an exhibit of human-body paintings, etc.

The sand ridge on the east and the expansive sand plateau on the west are called The East Sand and The West Sand, respectively. The East Sand is a cultural district, where the Yulin Middle School is located, from which many famous people have graduated. The other buildings there are mainly dwelling houses. In the newly-built West Sand area, there are office buildings, residential buildings and little iron-sheet sheds serving as shops dotting the slopes on both sides of the highway. From the highest points of The East Sand and The West Sand, one has a distant view of layers of cave dwellings, forests of chimneys much like tree trunks deprived of all their leaves. This quite inspired the imagination of one or two of the travelers: in the spring with the appearance of the new green of the willows and the flowers in a riot of color, could these trunks come to life? If they could, it must be moist fog instead of smoke coming out of them. While we travelers were walking ahead, we came in sight of the red cock flying off the high brick gateway, the white dog leaning against the low wall, and the cars coming and going to and fro in all directions. It was almost time for sundown, and people were all on their way home. On a long and steep slope of a road, girls were seen pushing their bicycles up, panting and sweating. The strenuous effort, however, made them even more charming by adding a rosy color to their jade-like cheeks. A young man on a motorcycle took no notice of the steep slope. With a step on the accelerator, he drove zooming past the girls proudly, leaving them all in a state of envy.

We travelers heard that the water of Yulin is of a special kind called "peach blossom water," which never has a bit of sediment when boiled and tastes better than the mineral water sold in bottles in big cities. When using the water to wash hair, one's hair becomes clean, smooth and glossy without the use of shampoo. People of the counties around Yulin have always sighed in envy: "How should such good water only favor Yulin, and not be found anywhere else?" Thanks to the good water, the bean curd made in Yulin is well-known for its tenderness and deliciousness. Accordingly, Yulin has many bean curd workshops. Within a space of one hundred meters, there usually are three or four such shops, each of which has several gigantic jars and a large pot with white cloth in the shape of a funnel hanging over it, used for filtering soybean milk. The Yulin people take a great fancy for the bean curd; their meal tables can be short of meat and vegetables, but not bean curd. In most cases, bean curd is not bought by money, but exchanged for beans. Customers usually come with a basin of soybeans or black soybeans and go back holding a large trembling chunk of steaming bean curd. The dagger used to cut the bean curd is made of golden, shining brass, which contrasts sharply with the white bean curd and makes the very act of cutting the bean curd an artistic performance. Like the stirring Yulin tune, whenever the Yulin bean curd is mentioned, people of the counties around Yulin are much delighted. They say that the Yulin bean curd seems to dissolve under one breath and that one bite of it is enough to make the eater fragrant all over for half a year. Days before the Spring Festival, highways leading to Yulin would be flooded with trucks containing pails, big or small, all for the same purpose of buying the Yulin bean curd.

Corruption in the present society is also an object of general condemnation in Yulin. However, the criticism is somewhat softened by the recognition that there was scarcely any bean curd in the recent past. Life is better than before. About a dozen years earlier, Yulin was famous not for bean curd, but for "steel-wire noodles," a kind of hard noodle made from corn, which was said to be very difficult to digest. At that time, when a tire was burst, people would say it must be pierced through by some lost remnants of "steel-wire noodles," which, they believed, were all-conquering. This kind of joke often provoked roars of laughter then, though it may sound a little bitter to today's ears.

Steel-wire noodles and bean curd are often regarded as the distinguishing marks of the different eras.

Placed on our meal table were milk, fish and mutton, all produced in the suburbs of Yulin, in addition to the bean curd. What was even more attractive was a specialty, at the first sight of which all travelers exclaimed, "Donkey hooves!" The hooves looked vivid and fresh as if they had just been cut off the donkeys and washed clean and served on plates, but when observed more closely, we travelers began to realize that they were actually fried pastries. Everyone was overjoyed with this discovery. The exact likeness and the name with local flavor kept us travelers delighted for several days.

As early as the Ming Dynasty (1368 – 1644), the Yulin people began to weave cloth with camel's hair. During the Jianjing and the Longqing periods in the Qing Dynasty (1644 – 1912), they paid tribute to the emperor with their camel-hair products. Later, they used sheep wool to weave blankets and carpets. Now blankets are turned out on a large scale with much modernized equipment and sold far and near, whereas carpets are still woven by hand. With tall factory buildings built and production updated, Yulin can produce one hundred thousand woolen blankets a year. Almost three out of ten of the aforementioned pretty girls work in blanket factories. Clever and deft, they weave into the blankets rosy clouds above the frontier city, the sprays in the Yuxi River, the noble spirit of the ancient generals, and the tender feelings of the Yulin popular music. In recent years the Yulin woolen blankets have not only been sold all over China, but also exported to many foreign countries. And there has always been greater demand than supply. Before the Spring Festival when the singers and dancers from Yulin created a great sensation in Moscow, the Yulin woolen blankets were displayed in the shop windows of the city and caused a purchasing rush among the Russians.

As the woolen blankets are so important for Yulin people, they have developed a habit of measuring a person's income by the blanket, hence the common saying "one-blanket cadre," for a cadre's monthly salary was just enough to buy a woolen blanket. In the past, a cadre's monthly salary was always in keeping with the price of a woolen blanket—when the salary was a little more than thirty *yuan*, the blanket was also a little more than thirty *yuan*, when the salary was raised to forty *yuan*, sixty *yuan* and then to one hundred, the price of the blanket rose accordingly, much to the cadres' indignation. In recent years, the price of the blanket has kept rising like a tall and straight poplar. Every new year finds a higher price. Today one blanket sells for one hundred and ninety *yuan* and there is word of another price increase in the near future. In contrast, a cadre's monthly salary, like a short sand willow, lingers at one hundred and ten or twenty[1]. It seems that the "one-blanket cadre" now can only own half a blanket or even less if the price rises again. This fact has caused a lot of sighs among people whenever it is mentioned. Similarly, the folk singers and dancers that amazed the Russians go from bad to worse economically. The actors and actresses find it more and more difficult to have their monthly salaries and their public medical expenses paid. As a result, more sighs have risen from the people.

Stepping out of the Yulin city and traveling towards the north, one would enter the realm described in the poem of Wang Wei (701 – 761), a famous Tang Dynasty poet: "In the desert a single column of smoke is rising straight, over the long river the round sun is falling fast." What a boundless desert! It was said that Wang Wei leaned on the great wall when writing this poem, otherwise, how could this section of the great wall be broken into several parts later?

The Yulin people say everyone in the city has to eat thirty-three liters of sand during his whole life. It is true that when the wind blows, sand flies about, beating one's brows and eyes and dancing into the mouth. The Yulin people, though often with grains of sand in their stomachs, have faced the desert bravely. The middle-aged guide with whiskers told us travelers proudly: "In the past, sand advanced and man retreated, but now man advances and sand retreats." These words contained the exceptional vigor and resolution that could also be found in Wang Wei's poems. Looking around, we travelers saw a variety of scattered bushes fastening the sand to the ground like rivets. The yellow and shining sand, intermingled with evenly distributed black bushes as it was still not time for them to turn green, formed a vast "modern" picture. This greatly inspired one of the travelers who suggested to the guide: "The natural scenery here really makes an original design for your carpets. It would surely please both the domestic and foreign customers and there should be no need of worrying about lack of good designers." "What an excellent idea!" the guide exclaimed, feeling as if a lamp in the heart had been lit. "We used to go to Xi'an to get an artist to make a design at the cost of thousands of *yuan*," he continued, "but then found it in poor taste. Now we can adopt a much better design right here and save money!"

Always far away from the capital, the Yulin people have been characterized as over-confident, unrestrained people, inclined to live freely and carry themselves with ease. It is true not only of the Yulin men, but also of the women. When staying in the hotel, we travelers often heard the woman attendants singing aloud. Even if they were twenty or thirty meters apart sweeping the corridor, they managed to talk to each other at the top of their voices. This was the way stamped in their nature, for they came from the vast desert or the expansive valleys. Although all these might be forbidden in most hotels, we travelers could feel no annoyance, only gratification. As we did not get a chance of hearing Yulin folk songs and watching the folk dances, this indeed was a satisfactory compensation since we found ourselves infused in an uninhibited aesthetic sense of vigor, gracefulness, enthusiasm, and dexterity when observing these women's tall, slim figures and their quick, seemingly deliberately overacted way of cleaning the rooms.

The translator's notes:

1. Cadres' one hundred and ten or twenty monthly salary only tells the salary level in late 1980s and early 1990s. Cadres' salary level is considerably raised to a few thousand *yuan* in 2010s.

About the author: Liu Chengzhang (1937 –) is a notable poet, essayist and has published quite a number of collections of essays. Many of his lyrical essays focus on Shaanxi Province of China, especially on Northern Shaanxi.

About the essay: This essay was written in April, 1989. It shows to some extent the author's vague, and therefore mild, criticism of the excessive focus on "getting rich" in China at that time, in addition to some description of people's dissatisfaction and disappointment that went hand in hand with the development in the 1980s. Traditions and popular culture in Yulin are also vividly presented.

The Song for the Gods

Zhou Tongbin

I always feel like singing a song dedicated to the gods, who, dressed in a riot of color, sweetened and brightened the narrow world of my childhood with their interesting stories. My companions and I did not really believe that the gods were something of great might, who could dictate man's fate, but only thought that they were beautiful and amusing.

I was just in my early teens at that time. Although I often saw the adults knit their brows and heave sighs for food and clothes, I knew nothing about the hardships in life. Whenever I returned home from the firewood-collecting and cattle-herding trips, I would invite some friends to go out and play together. However, in the small desolate village, we could find few places good for playing. On the highest point of an elevation covered with a luxuriant growth of grasses and dotted with star-like flowers at the east end of the village, stood a tiny temple housing the Village God. It was so small that it looked like a boundary stone from far away, and when examined closely, it was found to be only about five feet wide. On the elevated stand made of gray bricks rested a miniature house topped with green, glazed tiles in the shape of a mandarin duck. In the shady spot of it grew a motley of moss. The inside of the temple was just as big as a square table. In the middle was laid a one-foot statue of an old man with a white beard, dressed in a loose robe of yellowish brown and holding a dragon-headed walking stick in his hand. He looked very forbidding, as if he felt it beneath his dignity to speak to a mortal. What was exciting to us children about the Village God was that he had more than a dozen wives standing in line on both sides of him. According to the village lore, when someone fell ill, he or she should burn three joss sticks and make three kowtows before the Village God. If the patient got better later, he or she should go to the temple again to fulfill the vow previously made to the god. As it was said that the Village God was a lecherous old man and liked to have a lot of wives, one would have a clay woman figurine made and send it to the Village God to be his wife. All these women figurines were only as high as half a foot, but each was charmingly and prettily made, with different manners and expressions. There was the delicately pretty one, the naively simple-minded one, the swaying and slender one, the sickly listless one, and the one with knitted brows, the one with a heavy heart, the one with a flirtatious leer, the one with a bright smile, the one with coyly closing eyes... All were lifelike beauties! We children often climbed the brick stand and got into the temple. As it was too low for us to stand straight and too narrow for us to squat fully, we had to half stand and half squat with our buttocks tightly against the walls and let the Village God and his wives stay ignominiously under our hips. Then, we children would take up the wives of the Village God one by one and make comments on their looks just according to each other's own aesthetic standard. Sometimes, as we could not agree with one another about which one was more beautiful, we would shake our little fists at each other. After the appreciation of the woman figurines, we would arrange them in two lines and put the Village God in the place of a team leader; or we had the alternative of arranging them into square battle formation with the Village God sitting in the middle as a marshal. When we were tired of all this, we would ask silly questions to each other: "How could the Village God support so many wives?" "Does he have a bed big enough to hold all his wives and himself?" "Can his wives give birth to babies?" The questions were later brought up to the adults, who usually responded to them with a severe scolding or turned a deaf ear.

One day, when we were quite warmed up by our usual games in the temple, Grandpa Lump, a woman-like old bachelor, passed by the temple door and saw our mischievous tricks and his face turned very white. He exclaimed: "Oh, children! It is extremely sinful to do that, the Village God will let your eyes go wrong in order to punish you." On hearing this, we hurried to put the Village God and his wives to their normal places. Then having clapped off the joss dust on our hands, we climbed out of the temple and ran away like rabbits.

But what Grandpa Lump said did not come true. None of us developed eye disease. Whenever we had time, we still went to the temple to play. We did not believe that the Village God could punish anyone because we saw with our own eyes that the god and his wives were merely made of clay.

At the south corner of the west of the village, there was a solitary courtyard surrounded by a forest. The family that lived there did not engage in agricultural work but made a profession of molding gods from generation to generation and had been called "the artisan-painter's family" by the villagers. It was said that when there was still an emperor the then-living grandpa of the old artisan-painter was among the best ones of the trade and hence was summoned to Nanyang by the local authorities to make a statue of Kong Ming, a wise man who was entitled the Marquis of Wuxiang, at the temple specially built for him on the Mount of the Lying Dragon. He was generously rewarded for his masterly artistry. However, the crude wood door of the artisan-painter's family was always closed. We could not make out whether it was because they did not want the people to know the inglorious origin of the gods or because they did not want to be delayed in work by visiting people.

One day, the person in charge of the theatrical performance of a neighboring village came to the artisan-painter's home to "invite" the god. Following the strains of music accompanied by the sound of drumbeats and fireworks, my companions and I entered the courtyard with the throng of a-dult onlookers. We passed to and fro under the elbows of the adults and looked everywhere—at the courtyard and the house. In the middle of the front courtyard, there were several large vats made in Junzhou containing mud. Under the awning of the reed mats stood various gods or unfinished products of gods. Some were already painted colors and gilded and appeared to have been dressed in neat clothes and hats, some were simply figurines of bare clay, some only had their noses and pleats of the clothes made, some were still shapeless lumps of mud, some were just in the state of a board nailed to a club, with wheat straw tied around. All these things revealed the whole process of making the gods. On the windowsill were placed some figurines, finished or unfinished, which I immediately recognized to be the wives of the Village God. I fixed my eyes on them, comparing them with my memory of their likes in the temple to decide which was the most pretty and charming.

Inside the artisan-painter's house, the statues of gods could be seen everywhere. The Guanyin Bodhisattva sitting in the lotus throne quietly stayed in the nook of the door; the Horse King with a red face and three eyes stood back to back against the corner of the walls with the Ox King who had a big nose and long ears, and the great warrior Mr. Guan, holding his crescent-moon broadsword carved with a black dragon, was just lying under the bed. All the walls were occupied by pictures of gods, whose dresses, adornments, decorating bands and fluttering gown fronts together with the clouds around them were really pleasantly appealing though I could hardly figure out what they were supposed to take charge of respectively. On the long desk were laid a lot of bowls and small plates holding pigments and ink, and round containers filled with Chinese painting brushes. There was also a set of unfinished pictures: one was only a rough sketch drawn by the end of a joss stick; another had just been delineated with ink; the third had already been covered with paint of two light colors ... The old artisan-painter, silver-headed and of dark complexion, was expressionlessly drawing the brows of a god. I found that he resembled the Village God in the temple very much. Wasn't the god molded after the model of himself? Having seen the gods in molds of bare clay and on the paper, I began to realize that the gods were only used to make money by the artisan-painter's family and were not almighty at all. If they were as it was said, why didn't the artisan-painter's family members develop eye diseases for putting the gods in irreverent places?

The god, once laid in a special position, would really become a god.

In the middle of the back wall of the main room in our house, an altar was specially set for our ancestors and the gods. At one side, there was a piece of red paper bearing the words: "The sacrificial place for the ancestors of three generations," which was flanked by the two pieces of the couplet:

Offerings in the ancient containers can remind us of the Spring and Autumn Period;

The three cardinal guides and the five constant virtues will last thousands of years.

At the other side, the Kitchen God and his wife were flanked by a different couplet which reads as follows:

When the gods say good things in Heaven;

Luck and fortune fall to the world of the mortals.

The Kitchen God's picture, bought from the New Year's fair, was a piece of thin paper of block printing, very brightly colored. The god looked like a smiling stout old man, and his wife like a smiling plump old woman. They both appeared kind-hearted and always gazed at the people jubilantly. Whenever I had leisure, I would stand before the picture of the god and stare at it for a long time. Under my intent look, it seemed that the god and his wife opened their mouths and were ready to speak. Were they going to tell me an unheard story or to teach me an ancient song for children?

On the twenty-third of the twelfth lunar month, sacrifices were made for the Kitchen God to send him to the palace in Heaven to report to the Jade Emperor. White steamed buns made of refined wheat flour and sweets were displayed before the god's picture. I knelt before the altar holding a red cock, which was supposed to be the horse the god would ride on his trip to Heaven. My grandma mumbled beside me for some time mainly asking the Kitchen God to speak well of us before the Jade Emperor in order that the next year the rain would come more on time to ensure a better harvest and accordingly a better life. Staring at the white steamed buns and sweets, I had great fear that the god might eat some of the good things or take half of them away as the solid food for his trip to Heaven. In that case, I would have little of them left to eat. Hence, the first thing I would do the following morning was to steal a glance at the altar. I found all the white steamed buns and sweets were still where they had been.

"Why didn't the Kitchen God and his wife eat the buns and sweets?" I would ask grandma.

"The god has already known our minds," Grandma answered. "The offerings are usually eaten by human beings. Gods are satisfied by taking in the smell of them and don't really eat them. " I was glad to know the good things could be left untouched by the god. Seeing the smoke of the joss sticks curling upward and the paper ashes whirling up to the roof right after the sacrificial rites for the Kitchen God, I would look at the dark sky in wonder while imagining that the Kitchen God of my family and those of the neighboring families were all riding the "red horses" soaring steeply to the heaven. Meanwhile, I began to worry about where to tie all the horses since thousands of families had sent their kitchen gods to the Jade Emperor. Although the emperor's hall was spacious, yet how could it hold tens of thousands of Kitchen Gods? When all the kitchen gods spoke to the emperor, whom would he listen to? Could he remember all the things the kitchen gods reported to him? I asked grandma about all this but only received an angry glare from her. My curiosity ran further in this course: Did the Kitchen God rise to Heaven alone or with his wife? Could one cock carry two people at the same time? If he left his wife at home, did his wife feel lonely? I asked grandma again, who just said sternly: "Don't talk nonsense on these great occasions!"

On the first day of the first lunar month, not only the celebration of New Year's Day reached the peak, but the sacrificial rites for gods were also culminated. Gods could be found everywhere. Red pieces of paper, each bearing one god's name, together with joss sticks, could be seen on the millstones, door-stones, cloth-beating stones, the well terrace, the grinding-stone, the stone-roller, the carts, and on the big poplar whose trunk took two men's full arms joined together to surround. The most animated place was the height quite close to the temple for the Village God at the east end of the village, where the villagers set up a reed mat shed in which the sacrificial table was laid with a picture of gods hung above it. The Jade Emperor, who was also called The Heaven by the farmers, and the Fire God were both in the vertical scroll of painting. The Heaven was pictured dressed in a brocade robe and wearing the Chinese crown with jade strings hung before and behind on the head. Surrounded by brilliant air and clouds, he was sitting sanctimoniously over the Fire God, who, with red beard and a red fierce face, was dressed in red clothes and red hat and surrounded by flaming red fire. The most interesting thing was that the couplet on the two sides of the gods' painting did not bear words as usual, but had the Eight Immortals in a Chinese legend on them: Lü Dongbin, Han Xiangzi, He Xiangu, and Lan Caihe were on one side, and Zhang Guolao, Li Tieguai, Han Zhongli and Cao Guojiu on the other. The Eight Immortals all wore different expressions and manners: Lü Dongbin looked easy and comfortable; Han Xiangzi, natural and unrestrained; He Xiangu, elegant and beautiful; Lan Caihe, carrying the thin-necked gourd for wine, was still intoxicated and Zhang Guolao was leisurely on the back of a little donkey with a pink nose, pink eyes and four silver hooves... All of them, with their robes and sleeves floating in the air, looked as if they were speeding across the sky to the west by riding clouds and mist to attend the flat peach party[1] held by the Heaven Queen. While looking at the gods' pictures, we children asked each other in secret: Does The Heaven have a wife? Why didn't she come together with The Heaven to smell the offerings? Does the Fire God have a wife? Isn't she burned up when sleeping with a man surrounded by fire? We no longer dared to ask the adults about these questions for fear of being scolded again. All through this time, great quantities of joss sticks were burned in the shed and the whole place was enshrouded in dense smoke. All people of the village, rich or poor, had come to burn joss sticks. Each rich family burned bunches of joss sticks and every poor family could only offer three sticks. Fireworks were kindled to accompany each family's ceremony of burning joss sticks. The rich usually had huge strings composed of five hundred firecrackers, while the poor held very little strings made up of much smaller firecrackers. Anyway, the sound of the firecrackers like frying dried soybeans could be heard from morning to the evening on the height. We children ran there in a rush to pick up unlit firecrackers from the ground, and when meals were ready, the adults would call several times before we returned home reluctantly.

When the New Year's celebration was over, the gods' picture was taken away and the shed pulled down; only the temple for the Village God was left alone on the height. The spring that followed was dominated by a lack of grain. We only had rice chaff, edible wild herbs and grass roots,

173

and elm bark to cook as food, and we could often hear sighs from grandma and my parents. I thought maybe the kitchen gods of the rich families were more powerful because they were supplied with much more white steamed buns. Or was it because the rich families burned more joss sticks and kindled louder firecrackers that the Jade Emperor bestowed good fortune exclusively to them?

Before long, with the liberation of the country in 1949, I bid farewell to my childhood. The temple for the Village God on the height was torn down. People used the bricks from it to build up well terraces and made it more convenient for the villagers to draw water from the wells. Land was allotted to the family of the artisan-painter, and except his youngest son, who was assigned to the cultural center of the county to work as a painter, all the other members of the family began to do farm work. The picture with the Jade Emperor and the Fire God was nowhere to be found. My family kept making sacrifices to the Kitchen God and his wife for a while after the liberation. But later when our life was much better and my grandma and parents always wore smiles on their faces, the Kitchen God's picture in my family disappeared. Instead, the picture of Chairman Mao was respectfully hung in the middle of the back wall of the main room in our house.

The translator's notes:

1. "Flat peach party" is an allusion from a classic Chinese novel, *Pilgrimage to the West*. This party is said to be held once a year by the Heaven Queen to treat the heavenly deities with ripe, flat peaches.

About the author: Zhou Tongbin (1941 –) is a notable local essayist in Nanyang, Henan Province. He has published hundreds of essays, which mainly focus on his native province.

About the essay: This essay was written on July 24, 1981. In this essay traditional customs and trends of worship in different periods of China are mentioned.

The Barbershop Carried on a Shoulder Pole

Zhou Tongbin

In the village where I was born, there had never been a barbershop. It was only when I went to visit my maternal grandmother at an old town fifteen kilometers from my natal village that I saw one. The barbershop, with a tress of long hair hung high in front as the shop sign, was located at the corner of the crossroads. Inside the shop, there was a big chair whose back could be put into vertical or almost horizontal positions. This roused my curiosity in such a way that I stood near the door stealthily staring at the chair for a long time.

In my own village, the barber carried all his barber tools on a shoulder pole. Suspended at one end of the pole was a big copper pot, more than a foot high, over a wood-burning stove that kept the water in the pot warm. Hanging on the other end was a stool with a drawer under the seat, containing the old-fashioned straight razor, the whetstone, and the whetcloth. This has inspired the well-known allegorical description of unrequited love: "The hair-shaver's loads—hot only at one end."

The pockmarked barber, whose family name was Liu, lived on the bank of a river about a mile from my home. According to the silver-bearded

old man of our village, the Liu family had been barbers ever since the
Manchu People entered Beijing and took control of the whole country in
1644. From generation to generation, the family had been known as "hair-
shaver Liu," and the present successor, Pockmark Liu, was almost as famous as the richest man in the vicinity, Landlord Ruan. The difference
was that Landlord Ruan lived in an imposing dwelling with a spacious
courtyard behind a pitch-dark front gate, and was rarely seen while Pockmark Liu had to travel to our village and several others to provide his services each month. In summer, his pole-carried barber tools were put under
the Chinese honey locust by the pond in the center of our village. In winter, the place chosen would be the lee side of a house. On rainy or snowy
days, he would use the public mill. As a custom practiced from the ancient
time, no money was charged for hair-shaves, and every adult paid for the
service by giving the barber a liter of Chinese sorghum at harvest time. Also as a custom, adulthood was decided by state of marriage. Brother Da-
gui, for instance, married at the age of sixteen to a thirteen-year-old girl,
was therefore recognized as an adult and would have to pay a liter of sorghum. Conversely, Uncle Shuanzi, nearly thirty years old but still unmarried, was not regarded as an adult. Moreover, one adult could bring all his
unmarried sons to have free hair-cuts if they needed them. So it was that
the second Uncle Cheng, who had fifteen sons, just paid one liter of sorghum all the same. Third Uncle Tunzi who had no sons but only a daughter
(girls never had their hair shaved), was discounted not one grain of sorghum. Another custom was that the villagers should take turns to invite the
barber to meals on his service days in the village. Though the social status
of a barber was very low and he was not given the seat of honor at the din-

ner table, people in our village never looked down upon Pockmark Liu and always treated him as a relative because a great-grand-aunt in our village had married his great-grandfather. Every family, when the turn came to invite him to a meal, would manage to prepare four dishes: salted soy beans, shredded turnips dressed with sauce and vinegar, pickled green pepper and an omelet. One special rule was that if the barber was invited to give a hair-shave to a baby boy on the day when he was a month old, the meal table could be composed of chicken and wine. In addition, at the time the barber took his leave, money or presents wrapped in red paper would be given to him.

It was only Landlord Ruan who broke the old rule. When his grandson was one month old, he summoned Pockmark Liu to give the baby a head-shave. Then, instead of serving the barber a good meal, he sat him down with two of his hired farm laborers in the stable to eat steamed cornbread, fearing that Pockmark Liu's presence at his own table might harm his prospects of becoming even wealthier. This humiliating treatment angered Pockmark Liu, who afterwards cursed Landlord Ruan at every village he went to.

I always liked to watch hair shaving very much. Every time the barber came, there would be a crowd of children who stood looking on as if watching a wonderful performance. I always managed to get into the crowd and listened attentively to the interesting spiels of Pockmark Liu. One day, I remember, he talked about Landlord Ruan: "Behold the haughty bearing of the landlord! Fifty years ago when I shaved his head on his one-month day, I could not help but laugh at his pointed purple little head, exactly like a frosted eggplant, with only a few yellow hairs on it. Hahaha!" Then he added: "His father was even more ugly. In his younger years, he went to Shanghai and came back with eighteen ulcer scars on his head. I was summoned to shave the several hairs which still remained and given the order to keep the secret for him. I told him that the ulcer scars might break my razor and if I was not paid handsomely, then... Reluctantly he gave me a silver dollar. With the money I bought wine and meat, and gave my poor pals a good treat. After we drank to our hearts' content, I told them where I got the money. They all burst into a belly laugh. Hahaha!" On hearing this, the onlookers' laughter filled their eyes with tears. He himself laughed, too, and every pockmark on his face beamed. Meanwhile he just stood still, busily shaving, and from time to time he warned the person being served: "Don't move, or your head will be cut. "

According to the silver-bearded old man, men in ancient times did not have haircuts but coiled their hair into a bun at the top of their heads. In the Qing Dynasty (1644 – 1912), men had hair at the fore part of the head shaved and wore a braided pig-tail in back. With the founding of the Republic of China, the style changed and men began to have their heads clean shaved, like the Buddhist monks. It was said that the grandfather of Pockmark Liu once braided the plait of the grandfather of Landlord Ruan. In the process of combing, three hairs fell of the head, which was used by the old miser as a pretext to deny the yearly one liter of sorghum for three years on end.

When the business was handed down to Pockmark Liu, men no longer wore pig-tails, so he had only to devote himself to head-shaving. For the children there were several ways of wearing their hair. Most of them wore some hair above the forehead in the shape of a crescent moon; the more pampered had the top and the back of the head shaved, leaving a ring of short-cut hair, which looked very much like a sunflower. Children of the most squeamish parents usually had a tress of hair left unshaved above the left ear, called "the turtle's tail." The grandson of Landlord Ruan wore his hair in this way. Every time he followed the accountant of his family to collect the rents, we children would surround him and compete to tug at his "turtle's tail." As the hair was deliberately left for others to pull in order to avoid disasters and catastrophes, the child dared not tell his grandpa no matter how much he suffered from all the other children's pulling.

I was always afraid of being shaved. Every time I was asked to get my hair done, I would nervously approach the barber, fearing that one of my ears might some day be shaven off. In contrast, Pockmark Liu was always smiling and told me in great earnestness: "By my village there is a river. On both banks of the river there is a lot of stone. Inside the stone cracks there are some crabs, which move sideways and each of them has eight legs. They are really interesting creatures. Next time I come, I'll bring a few of them to you. Do you know how to catch crabs? ..." Usually before he reached the topic of how to catch crabs, he would have finished the shaving. So with a pat on my back, he would say: "Now, get out of here." With this he would proceed to shave the head of another child and began the same story all over again. Although he never brought any crabs to us children as he had promised, we always hoped when listening to his old story that next time he would bring us the interesting creatures with eight legs, while forgetting all about the sharp razor moving on our heads.

Pockmark Liu had no son but he did have a daughter. The folks began to worry about the continuation of the service and about whether they would have to be "long-hair men" if something happened to the old barber. Seeing the hair on his temples more and more white and his back more and more bent, people grew more and more anxious.

In late spring when the chinaberry was in blossom, Pockmark Liu came one morning after breakfast with a girl in her late teens, who carried the loaded shoulder pole for the old man. As soon as the loads were put down under the Chinese honey locust by the pond in the center of the village, the villagers gathered automatically around them. The girl, as pretty as a flower, wore a thick braid about three feet long and had ten delicately thin fingers. Pockmark Liu announced: "I'm now too old to stand steadily. From today on, my daughter Meizi will shave heads for you. The girl is still young, and I'd like to beg your pardon in advance for any fault she might commit. Since we are now liberated (referring to the foundation of People's Republic of China—the translator) and the government calls for equality between men and women.... " With those words, he bowed deeply to the villagers. Tears could be seen in his eyes. Up to that time, people had never heard of a woman barber. It must have been very hard for the old man to have made such a decision. However, Meizi turned out to be a very skillful hand from the very beginning. The adults said that her shaving was just like a cool, gentle wind blowing over the head. Children were no longer afraid of hair-shaving and even vied with each other to be shaved earlier. It was said that before taking the service over, she shaved gourds for two full months at home. Two razors were worn out because of her continual practice. What was more, within one month, she shaved her father's head thirty times. What an assiduous girl she was!

After the first round of services led by her father, Meizi began to tour alone. The folks liked her very much. Whenever she arrived, old grannies and young matrons would come up and talk about everything with her while doing their needlework. At the meal time, the elderly women competed to invite her and made dumplings or fried pancakes especially for her. Several young men, attracted by the prettiness of Meizi, insisted that their faces should be shaved after the head-shave. As the only available seat was the low stool, the customers must turn their faces upward to be shaved. On such occasions, the elderly men would keep their eyes closed; whereas these young ones opened their eyes as wide as possible and looked smiling-ly and affectionately at the girl's fair face only half a foot away. Meizi, much embarrassed and annoyed, pursed up her lips. The silver-bearded old man happened to arrive to have a hair-shave and saw all this. He stern-ly reprimanded the young men: "You immature boys are just like half-grown asses. There's still a long time before you have the need of shaving the fine soft hair on your faces. Remember, you unmarried boys are forbid-den to have face-shaves—it's our old rule!" Then he turned to the girl: "If they insist on your shaving their faces again, just shave off their brows!" After that time, these young men never dared to ask for another face-shave.

When I grew older, I left my home village to go to school and did not come back often. I heard that in order to continue to serve the folks in the vicinity, Pockmark Liu married his daughter to a young fellow who was willing to move into the bride's house, going against the usual practice of sending the daughter over to the groom's family. The couple's married life was happily spent with the groom staying at home doing the farm work and the bride making service tours. Later, when I returned home, I saw Meizi busy shaving under the Chinese honey locust. Beside the deep copper pot boiling the water stood a handsome boy, now feeding the stove with pieces of wood, now passing some water or a towel to Meizi. I was told that he was the son of Meizi. Then I inquired about her father and the villagers answered with a sigh: "His grave mound has already been overgrown by grass. "

My grandma told me that my father's one-month-old shave was done by the father of Pockmark Liu and my one-month-old shave was given by Pockmark Liu himself. Days ago I received a letter from home and learned that my wife had given birth to a baby boy. I was back home on the day when my son was one month old. As luck would have it, it was Meizi who shaved the head of my son. Only the shaving was no longer done under the Chinese honey locust or on the lee side or in the mill, but in the newly-built barbershop with the big chair and an electric fan, where Meizi, who already had some wrinkles at the eye corners and silver hairs on the head, used electric hair-clippers instead of the old-fashioned straight razor to give my son the haircut. The thought suddenly came upon me: years later my son's son might be given the one-month-old haircut by the son of Meizi.

So long as there are men, there is the need for haircuts. We'll never forget the Liu family that has served us for so many years.

The translator's notes:

About the author: Zhou Tongbin (1941 –) is a notable local essayist in Nanyang, Henan Province. He has published hundreds of essays, which mainly focus on his native province.

About the essay: This essay was written in 1983. In this essay, not only the life and service of a barber and his family in the rural area of central China are described, but also the change of hair style in China all through the history is more or less mentioned.

The Dining Place Under the Tree

Zhou Tongbin

City people usually stick to the formal way of having meals around a table. Even if there might only be a dish of salted turnip or a few cloves of sweetened garlic as the available dishes to be had with rice, buns or noodles, the whole family will sit around the meal table to eat together. The farmers seldom observe such rites. When meals are ready, the old mistress will eat before the kitchen range, the daughter-in-law will hold her meal bowl and sit on the stone for beating cloth in the courtyard, or feed a child while eating in the shade of a tree in front of the house door. Unmarried girls eat silently in their own rooms and men eat outdoors. More often than not, there is a regular dining place in a village.

A great old willow grows in front of the house door of Number Eight Great Grandfather, covering in shade about six hundred square meters of the open ground. The shade makes the place fairly cool in summer, though it is warm in winter with the advantages of being both out of the wind and exposed to the sun. On days there is slight rain, the tree, in full-leaf, serves as a great umbrella, under which one can hear the sound of rain but cannot feel any raindrops. Owing to all of these advantages, this place has long been a regular dining spot of the village. Despite the fact that there are three or four bird nests in the tree and the sound of birds chirping can always be heard, never has one bit of the birds' wastes dropped into anyone's meal bowl. Many of the tree's roots swell out of the ground, undulating and zigzagging like snakes crawling in the mud. These roots, cleaned by wind and rain, and polished by frequent friction, make good seats for the diners. One branch of the roots in the north makes three curves and is the favorite of Number Eight Great Grandfather, who has squatted on it for scores of years, there taking his meals. The roots remain the same every year, not thicker, not disfigured, whereas he, alas, has turned from a boy into an old man of eighty.

Having a neat and quick wife who always had meals ready before other families, the Fifth Grandpa Kui would be the first to come to the dining place holding an enormous bowl of thick porridge with pickled Chinese cabbage piled on it and two steamed buns strung on the chopsticks, covered with minced dried red pepper soaked by hot oil. Then the other men, old or young, would arrive one after another, bringing with them their respective meals, say, noodles, maize or millet gruel, green gram soup, fried rolls with green onion, pancakes, steamed corn bread, steamed buns stuffed with vegetables, shredded radish, fermented soy beans, garlic juice, meat cured by salting, strong-smelling preserved bean curd, green onion dressed with sauce... The variety of food made the dining place almost as good as an exhibit of farmers' home-made meals.

Their wives' virtues were best reflected in the meal bowls of the husbands. The wife of Uncle Dog was very good at making thin, long, and pliable noodles. To eat them, Uncle Dog would first hang them about one foot above the bowl with chopsticks as if to examine them before sending them to his mouth with much proud noise. The Seventh Grandma Yao was quite a hand at making "the one-thousand-layer-cake" in the shape of a lotus leaf. The surface of the cake was oily, yellow and crisp with frying, but the inner layers were tender and delicious. Every time the Seventh Grandpa Yao brought some cakes to eat at the dining place, the others would look on in great envy and with mouths watering. The Second Grandpa Qing married a Sichuan woman who cooked rice in the very best way—she never made it too hard or too soft by putting too little or too much water and always managed to retain the rice's delicate fragrance. Holding a big bowl with rice piled like a snow mountain, the Second Grandpa Qing used to praise his wife while eating: "Though my wife is no tailor, she has given birth to a male baby and is so good at cooking..." The wife of the Monkey liked good food and once cooked eggs in the soup of fine dried noodles just for herself. After eating them, she did not bother herself with cleaning the pot, but directly made gruel of sorghum powder for her husband. When he arrived at the dining place the others found one piece of noodle in his gruel, and laughed: "How can your wife make only one noodle at a time?" The Monkey, in his embarrassment, hastened to cover it up: "I don't like noodles, but she insisted that I should at least have a little. " This forced pretext only provoked louder laughter. Lao Han had a slovenly wife, who either steamed bun bread too hard or overcooked everything. Hair and sticks were often found in what she had made. Hence Lao Han always tried to eat at the edge of the dining place as if he feared being detected.

The Fifth Grandpa Kui was always the last to leave the dining place. It was not because he had bad teeth and ate too slowly but because he had wide experience and talked too much. Having worked as a sedan carrier in his youth, he was fond of telling the others about his experience of carrying the wedding sedan for the third daughter of Landlord Ruan and about the

187

ostentation and extravagance of the families of both the bride and the bride-groom. He would describe their way of carrying the wedding sedan—an alternation of three quick steps, three slow steps, striding steps, minced steps, crossed steps—which completely dazed the bride sitting inside. Whenever this was mentioned, he would put down his bowl, on which laid the chopsticks with the steamed buns, and give a performance of his former trade until the Fifth Grandma Kui, who had been waiting to wash the pot and bowls, came to hurry him up as to get him finish his meal.

Private matters were usually not the topics of the dining place talks, with only one exception—the odd scandals about Lao Kuang. It was said that one year when he was in power he received as presents a tableful of parcels of pastry. But when the parcels were unwrapped one by one to be enjoyed, it was found that two of them contained donkey dung. He did not immediately make a scene about it, but later on during a mass meeting of the village, he alluded to this incident as an attack of the leadership of the Communist Party from the enemy class. At another time, Lao Kuang went to attend a banquet in a neighboring village. He was soon drunk and went out to look for the latrine. In his drunkenness he mistook the host's kitchen for the latrine and urinated into a pot of boiling water. Without knowing this, the host made tea with that very boiling water. After drinking some tea, Lao Kuang sobered up a little and remembered what he had done. Realizing that the tea was made with the water into which he had urinated, he vomited out all the meat and wine he had just had. It was a good thing that none of his family members ever came to eat at the dining place and that none of those who were present would tell him about it. Lao Kuang never knew that these malicious anecdotes served as spices to his fellow farmers.

Occasions sometimes occurred when the Fifth Grandpa Kui lost his monopoly in talking at the dining place. Shuanzi, a demobilized soldier, talked for several days during meals about the farmers in the south, who regarded the toads, snakes, and earthworms as delicious food, and the new foreign-style buildings they lived in. Even the grass they grew in their courtyards was imported. They went to Hong Kong fairs, and shopped in Guangzhou city, where they lived in hotels whose single bed cost a hundred *yuan* for one night. Uncle Dog had visited a brother-in-law working in a big city and returned to tell the villagers that the skirts the city women wore were very short; one could see everything beneath if the wind blew up their skirts. And there were offices introducing would-be spouses; the offering of a five *yuan* fee and two photos of oneself would enable one to find a partner in marriage. Even the old women over sixty registered in such offices to look for proper spouses... All these things were certainly much more interesting than the old yarns of the Fifth Grandpa Kui.

The atmosphere around the dining place was always gay and pleasant; hence, every meal, good or bad, became much more delicious for the resorters. If any of them missed one chance of eating there, he would be in low spirits. Two misses could reduce his appetite greatly and three misses might make it hard for him to eat dainties of any kind. The carpenter, though being a lame old man and living in the willow forest outside of the village, would walk with a stick at each meal time to the dining place. The blind Seventh Grandpa Wang could not work, but never failed to grope his way while holding his meal to join the others under the tree. The Seventh Grandpa Yao once sneaked out from the wedding feast of his daughter to the dining place and got severely scolded by his wife. Uncle Dog became much emaciated owing to the fact that he had to wait on his wife during her confinement in childbirth and was unable to have meals under the great old willow for one month. The Fifth Grandpa Kui once went to town to visit his daughter and was invited to stay by the family. At every meal he was served meat and wine. However, instead of enjoying their hospitality and the delicious food, within two days he developed homesickness, sick for the simple meals and the village dining place. Day by day, he grew so sick that he could hardly eat and sleep. At last he returned to the village without taking leave of his daughter's family.

In the past several years, though the great old willow is still as exuberant as ever, the attendants under it have become fewer and fewer. At first, it was the Fifth Grandpa Kui who took to his bed and never left it again until he was gathered to his fathers. With the eternal absence of the greatest talker among all the regular diners, the cheerful atmosphere much enjoyed by all participants is greatly diminished, to the everlasting regret of everyone. Next, the Second Grandpa Qing and the old carpenter respectively went to their resting places. Then, after having a nasty tumble, the Seventh Grandpa Yao caught hemiplegia and has since been confined to bed. Later, Uncle Dog left the village and started a bean-curd shop in town. As money has a greater gravitational force than the village dining place, he has seldom been seen to return. Shuanzi, since having married, has preferred eating intimately with his wife—putting food into each other's mouths—to going to the dining place. The Monkey has opened a grocery and is often too busy to go there. The other young men have now cultivated the habit of watching TV during meals... Only Number Eight Great-grandfather still squats over the three-curved roots eating his every meal, but the food no longer tastes as good as before. Seeing that the former gaiety has gone and the dining place lasting for scores of years has declined, he can do nothing but sigh despondently, "Ay..."

The translator's notes:

About the author: Zhou Tongbin (1941 –) is a notable local essayist in Nanyang, Henan Province. He has published hundreds of essays, which mainly focus on his native province.

About the essay: This essay was first written in October, 1987, then revised in January, 1989. In a lot of places in the countryside of central China, people had the tradition of eating their daily meals outdoors, not at any outdoor table, but by squatting at any place they preferred since their meals were usually simple and could be held in one or two big bowls. This kind of tradition began to change from late 1980s owing to the reasons mentioned in the last paragraph of this essay. This is also a change of the popular culture in the countryside of central China.